HER CYBORG COMMANDER

SUSAN HAYES

SUSAN HAYES

Her Cyborg Commander (Book 9 of the Drift: Haven Colony)

First Print: March 2025

Editor: Amanda Brown

Published by: Black Scroll Publications Ltd.

ABOUT THE BOOK

Coming to Haven colony should have marked the start of her new life, but the past isn't done with her yet.

River had negotiated the agreement that brought the survivors of Reamus Station to Haven. Back then, she'd dreamed it would be a sanctuary for her cyborg brethren, somewhere out of reach from those who had created and tormented them. She'd been wrong.

Now her home, her friends, and the future she's worked so hard for are all in danger... because of her.

He'd vowed to protect every cyborg in Haven... but he'd take on the galaxy to keep *her* safe.

Edge doesn't have any illusions about who or what he is—

a weapon forged in the heat of battle and quenched in the blood of his kills.

As happy as he is for the rest of his brethren to settle into new lives, he can't see himself doing the same. It's enough for him to watch over them from a distance, especially when it comes to River. She's beautiful, frustratingly stubborn, and far too good for him.

When an old enemy threatens their new home, these broken souls will have to decide which rules are worth breaking and which chances are worth taking.

This book is dedicated to Craig. For all you are. For all you do. For saying "I do." For being the hero in my own love story.
This story is also for Rosie. She knows why.

PROLOGUE

Beyond the edge of civilized space is a newly colonized planet. It's a haven for the homeless, the hopeful, and those dreaming of freedom.

The beings who live here might be different species from vastly different worlds - but they all have one thing in common. Whoever they are, and wherever they came from, Haven is now their home.

The land is uncharted. The dangers are unknown. It's a world full of possibilities – for those willing to risk everything.

Welcome to Haven Colony.

"Does anyone have any questions before we begin?" River asked the six cyborgs who sat waiting for their turn to be scanned.

"Yeah, I do. Why do we have to do this? We've been tested before and they didn't find anything."

She recognized the voice immediately. Of course Thrash would be the one to ask that question. The cyborg had never met a requirement he didn't want to challenge.

"It's not the same thing. Last time, we were scanned to detect rogue code and behavior mods." She touched her chest and looked straight at Thrash. "You know why we did that and what we learned. Three of us were involuntarily implanted with commands that made us vulnerable to outside influence."

The words tasted bitter as she uttered them. "Vulnerable to outside influence," was a prettier way of saying she and two of her friends had been turned into unwitting puppets under the control of their greatest enemy. The Gray Men might have been destroyed, or at least sent into hiding, but their influence over the cyborgs they'd created still held.

"And this time?" Thrash asked.

She shot him a look of mild annoyance. "I explained it two minutes ago. If you weren't paying attention, check your data storage and replay it."

A round of subdued laughter followed along with several jokes at Thrash's expense.

Once she had everyone's attention again, she continued, "This won't take long, and I promise it will be painless. In fact, I'm going to do it first, as a sort of demonstration."

Skye scowled at her from the other side of the room. *"I thought I was doing the demo this time? You don't have to do them all yourself."* The other cyborg sent via their internal comm channel.

"Next time it's your turn," she replied.

Skye's lips quirked into a brief, sardonic smile. *"That's only because you have to attend a council meeting this afternoon."*

River didn't reply. Everyone knew today was her last day as a member of Haven's leadership council. She'd already talked it through with everyone whose opinion mattered to her, and her decision was final. She'd done her duty and kept the promise she'd made what felt like a lifetime ago. It was time for her to move on to something else.

Shoving that thought aside, she focused on the task at hand. It only took a minute for her to activate the device she'd use today. Identical systems had been installed at various med-centers and communal buildings around the colony. Everyone in Haven was required to undergo the scan. It was the only way to be certain no other doppelgangers—physically perfect clones being controlled by a digitized consciousness that could be uploaded into the body—were hiding among the population.

For most of Haven's citizens, the scan would look for any indication of cloning or the presence of a bio-matrix made up of their own genetic material that acted as a repository for the digital consciousness that piloted the body. The cyborgs would have their coding scanned, with the results compared to their previous records. Any anomalies, no matter how small, would be investigated.

They had to be sure no more infiltrators were hiding in the colony.

River sat down beside the scanner and attached the sensors with an efficiency that came from practice. They'd been at this for several days now. A few more sessions and all the cyborgs would be done. As relieved as she would be once they'd all been cleared, part of her wished she could do this every day. The repeated scans reassured her that no one had tampered with her code— that she had her free will back and couldn't be used against her fellow cyborgs or the rest of the colony.

It would be hard to go back to the uncertainty.

When her demonstration ended, she detached the sensors and prepped the area for her next patient while Skye organized the group with a careful mix of encouragement and authority.

None of them wanted to be here. Testing like this

always stirred up memories every cyborg on the planet did their best to ignore. They all had scars from their time at Reamus Research Station, some more than others, but none of them had escaped that place without a lifetime's worth of nightmares.

By the time the last member of this group had been scanned, River's stomach was growling. Her hope that no one noticed was blasted to moon dust when Skye cleared her throat and gave her a knowing look. "*When was the last time you ate?*"

Cyborgs like them didn't need to eat regularly, thanks to the medi-bots they all carried. The nanotech could keep them at optimal performance levels for days even without food, rest, or medical attention. That didn't mean they could carry on without the basics of life indefinitely, though.

"*It's been a while,*" River sent back. Now that she thought about it, she couldn't recall the last time she'd eaten a proper meal. She had to check her data files to work out when she'd last eaten. The answer surprised her. Three days. *Qarf.* No wonder she was hungry. She hadn't stopped to eat or get a decent amount of sleep since they'd discovered they'd been infiltrated by the Shadows.

Neither of them said anything else until they were alone. Less than thirty seconds after the last of the group left, Skye stood in front of her with one hand on her hip and a look that would send a *gharshtu* running for cover.

"You and I are going to grab lunch now. There will be carbs, and chocolate, and no claims you are too busy."

River laughed. "Yes, ma'am."

Skye's expression softened, but she kept her hand planted on her hip. "Are you okay?"

It took her a moment to answer. "Sort of." River tapped her chest and then her temple. "All of this stirred up everything again."

"For me, too. How the *fraxx* are we supposed to heal and move on if those bastards won't leave us alone?" Skye asked, her voice raw. "Haven't they taken enough from us already?"

"Sometimes I wonder if they'll ever stop. First, it was the corporations. Then we learned there was a faction called the Gray Men who called the shots. Now the Grays have evolved into the Shadows. Every time we think they're gone, they come back as something worse."

The two of them lapsed into silence for several seconds, both caught up in memories of the past. River and Skye had suffered some of the same abuses, and they'd both been used as involuntary sleeper agents.

"We'll outlive every last one of the bastards," Skye declared.

"And then we'll dance on their graves," River said.

Skye nodded sharply and gripped River's shoulder. "Damn right we will. But first, we're going to get something to eat. They don't get to rob of us anything else... especially not Inet and Gali's cooking."

"Death first," River agreed. "Does that mean we're going to Earthly Delights? I love that place. Don't tell anyone I said this, but their cheese toast is even better than the Bar None." River's stomach rumbled at the mention of one of her favorite comfort foods.

"Your secret is safe with me."

Skye's easy words settled something inside River. Her friend was right. They couldn't live in fear all the time. If that happened, they had already lost the fight. That wasn't how her story ended. It couldn't be. But before she could start her new life, she had one more thing she needed to do. It was time to attend her last council meeting and hand back the responsibility she'd been given the day the others had chosen her to represent them. She'd found them a new home and a chance at a new life. Now, it was time she made a life of her own.

2

Why did leadership come with so many *fraxxing* meetings? Edge asked himself that question often, but so far he hadn't come up with a satisfactory answer. His cynical side insisted it was so the bigwigs could hear themselves talk, but in his rare moments of generosity, he admitted that none of the colony's leaders were much for grandstanding. There was so much work to do, and all of it required a nauseating amount of communication.

He sat in his usual place with his back to the wall furthest from the door. The table was round to allow everyone an equal position as well as a decent view of each other and anything displayed on the holo-projector that took up the center of the space.

The other members of the council arrived one or two at a time, claiming their seats without more than a few words of greeting. Exactly thirty seconds before the meeting was scheduled to start, River arrived. It was unusual for her to cut it so close. Normally, she was one of the first ones here, greeting the others with a smile and a bit of light banter before they got down to work. She never did that with him, though. Her smiles were reserved for other beings. The ones she wasn't afraid of.

The thought stung, but it was an old, familiar pain, easily ignored. At least, that's what he told himself. So what if she thought he was dangerous? She wasn't wrong about that. Though he resented her for telling the humans not to wake him and the other male cyborgs until after they'd arrived at the colony. She'd made them out to be monsters, too violent and unstable to be allowed any say in their future. By the time he and the others woke from cryo, it was too late to do anything but go along with the deal she'd made with the Vardarians.

Edge's gaze drifted to where Prince Tyran sat in quiet contemplation. In the beginning, he'd thought of the prince as the warden of the cyborgs' new prison. Now, he knew differently. The cyborgs were as much a part of the colony as any other citizen. It still rankled him that River had taken the choice away from him and the others... even if she had found them a safe place to call home.

River took the last remaining chair, which put her directly across the table from him.

Her short, dark hair was pushed back from her face, and the shadows beneath her eyes and lines at the corners of her mouth told him she was pushing herself too hard. Even cyborgs needed downtime, but River never took time for herself. She was always too busy taking care of everyone else.

The first time he'd seen her was as he and several other cyborgs were dumped into the general population area of Reamus Research Station. They'd all been "re-acquired" by their former masters despite the promises to free every cyborg in existence. Angry, injured, and weakened by their minimal diet, it was all he and the others could manage to stay on their feet. River had been the first to approach. When she'd smiled at him, her brown eyes full of kindness and her voice as gentle as a whisper, he'd felt something so unexpected he'd almost laughed aloud—peace. For one brief, shining moment, she made him feel at peace.

He'd known then that she was the best of them, and he'd continued in that belief until he'd woken up on Haven and learned what she had done while he'd been asleep. After all the nights he'd guarded her, after all the beatings he'd endured to protect her and the other females from the predations of the guards... she'd sold them into a new kind of slavery.

At least, that's what he'd thought back then, and his anger had made him say things he regretted. Not that he'd admit that to anyone. Especially not to her.

It was easier to leave things as they were.

It might sting that she was afraid of him... but that's only because she didn't know the truth. His soul was so much darker than she knew. If she had any inkling of the things he dreamed of doing to her? Stars above and below, she'd have fled the planet rather than risk staying anywhere near him.

His moment of reverie ended as Tyran rapped his knuckles three times on the table to call the meeting to order.

"We've got a lot to talk about today, and I know we've

all got things we need to be doing to finish securing the colony," the prince said. "We'll go around the table. Everyone give a brief summary of what you're doing and what you've learned. I'll start."

The Vardarian prince provided a concise report of what his spymaster had learned since their last meeting. It wasn't much, but it did confirm the identity of the two Vardarians who had been murdered and replaced with what he thought of as infiltration units. Some of the others called them doppelgangers, but most referred to them as ghosts. He didn't like either name. They added a sense of the supernatural to the situation, stoking everyone's fears. A frightened population was prone to making bad decisions. If that happened? Everything could go to hell in a rocket-powered handcart.

Around the table they went, each summarizing what they were working on and what they knew. Most of it he was already aware of, but he filed away every detail for later review, anyway. When Zanyr spoke, Edge gave the Vardarian his full attention. The male had been in the middle of the situation from the beginning. If anyone had anything new to add, it would be him.

Zanyr began by announcing that his mate Jenna had fully recovered from the attack that had nearly killed her. Everyone brightened at that, with smiles and words of encouragement easing the tension. The moment didn't last, though, as Zanyr briefed everyone on the details leading up to the discovery that they had been infiltrated.

Once Zanyr finished, Raze was the next to speak. "Your *mahaya* was a spy for our side? Why weren't we told about this? I thought this council was supposed to be kept apprised of everything important." The big cyborg managed to keep his voice calm, but there was no missing the anger behind his words.

"I had the same reaction," Zanyr replied. "But think about it for a minute. The more beings who knew, the more likely it was that someone would make a mistake. The fact none of us treated her any differently is why she was able to keep up the façade as long as she did. I don't like it any more than you do, but it makes sense." His voice dropped to a growl. "And if she ever does anything like that again, Torren and I will tie her to the damned bed and never let her leave the house without us."

That statement triggered an outburst of laughter and hearty agreement from every male present.

"I still don't like it," Raze grumbled when the laughter faded. "Once we start keeping secrets, where does it end?"

"We have to trust each other," River stated softly. "As much as we can, anyway. We're all here because we want Haven to thrive. Sometimes, that might mean we have to keep secrets."

"And who decides what to reveal and what to keep hidden?" Edge asked. "Vardarians? The humans? Who?"

River's deep brown eyes fixed on him. "We do. That's what this council is for. To make sure our decisions reflect the needs of the entire colony."

She was right, but it still rankled him for some reason. Probably because he had trust issues the size of a small planet and wasn't good at sharing responsibility. At least, that's what River had told him once, long before they were free.

Zanyr waited for a heartbeat before continuing. "So, in summary, we know the Shadows are behind this infiltration. The good news is that if they are still trying to introduce spies, they're not getting the information they want any other way. Whatever they're after, they haven't gotten it."

"Yet," Denz added. "They haven't gotten it yet. But they will keep trying. Obviously, they view the Vardarians as a threat to their control over this part of the galaxy. They don't want the races here forming alliances with anyone who might disrupt the status quo."

"You mean anyone who might cut into their profit margins," the Vardarian prince said, his tone drier than moon dust.

Denz nodded. "And that. But it's about more than money. We don't know who the new players inside the Shadow organization are, but the Gray Men were all corporate owners or high-level executives trying to gain the upper hand. Control means everything to those kinds of beings—not only the flow of wealth but resources and manpower. Haven represents something vastly different, and I don't think they want anyone else to try and replicate what we're building here. They need us to fail, and they'll do everything in their power to make that happen."

Edge hadn't intended to speak, but he couldn't stop the words from coming. "So, what you're saying is the corporations are coming after us. Again. And we're playing defense. Again. When is it our turn?" he demanded, scanning the faces around the table. "Or should I say, when is it *your* turn? Because none of the cyborgs are allowed to leave the planet. Not even to defend our *fraxxing* home."

To his surprise, no one tried to interrupt, so he kept talking. "We need to do something more than sit here and wait for them to come after us again. They're applying pressure to all our weak spots, waiting for something to break. Eventually, it will, and then what? We react to yet another emergency. I'm tired of *reacting*. First it was the raids to steal tantalum from this planet before we could mine it ourselves.

"Once we activated the security net around the planet, they tried messing with us in other ways: with spies from Earth, with nanotech designed to weaken the Vardarians. Then it was the Vardarian *Liq'za* and their intolerance for anything other than total racial purity. Now we've got operators wandering around in cloned bodies. What's next?"

Zanyr cleared his throat but didn't speak until Edge nodded his way and asked, "What else do you know?"

"I don't *know* anything, but I think someone has been messing with the machinery at my farm. The coordinates I programmed for one field shifted slightly, so some of the seed ended up in the ground too rocky for it to grow decently. Water is going to the wrong field, flooding out some areas and making others too dry. Bugs happen, but this season it feels like they're happening too often. I didn't put the pieces together until the last few days."

Several councilors spoke at once, but Tyran's voice carried over the others. "You've got enough to do already.

Can you hand the investigation off to someone else? Someone you trust to find the answers without triggering more rumors?"

"Already done," Zanyr replied.

Edge growled in frustration. "This is what I'm talking about. We're running around, putting out fires instead of making a move of our own."

"We're all in this together," Phaedra spoke for the first time. The prince's human consort wasn't officially part of the council, but she attended most meetings and spoke up for the human contingent until the first elections were conducted.

He turned to look her way and did his best to stay outwardly calm. The last thing he wanted to do was to set off Tyran's protective instincts. Not to mention the fact the little fuchsia-haired human female was slightly terrifying in her own right. "I know that. But if this goes sideways, *you* can find another world to call home. The cyborgs can't go anywhere. If we lose this place, we lose *everything*."

Raze slapped the table with an open hand. "*Fraxx* that. We're not losing to those void-sucking bastards. This has been my home far longer than any of you, and I'm not leaving. So long as I draw breath, the cyborgs have a home—one we'll defend together."

Edge was caught between gratitude for his brethren's words and surprise Raze had said so much in one go. The male could go for an entire meeting without uttering more than an occasional grunt.

"None of us are leaving," Tyran said. "Edge, I heard what you said. It is time we did things differently." The prince looked around the table, his expression serious. "We need to open the armories and arm Haven's citizens. I know most of us are already armed in some fashion, but that won't be enough if there's a real attack."

Edge sat back in his chair and tried to process what he'd heard. The armories contained body armor, combat gear, and tactical weapons. Enough to ensure every adult on the planet was outfitted for battle. One of the first decisions they'd made as a council was to keep the armories locked until there was an undeniable threat.

Holy *fraxx*, Tyran had heard him. More than that, he agreed. If the others felt the same way...

River shook her head, shooting down Edge's hopes before they even got off the ground. "Not until we're finished scanning everyone. The last thing we need is to arm our enemies before we know who they are."

Frustrated, he snapped at her. "You mean the scans you've spent the last few days performing on the cyborgs? The ones that don't mean a *fraxxing* thing because we already know none of us have been compromised? It's impossible because while a cyborg clone might look the same, they wouldn't have the same implants or internal comm-channels. We'd know if one of ours was replaced with an infiltration unit."

River's eyes narrowed, and he saw the flash of pain as his words landed like physical blows. "You'd think so, but we've already established that some of us *were* compromised. I—we can't be sure." She tapped her temple with a trembling finger. "We can't take our security for granted, because some of us have already had it taken away."

Angry at himself for starting them down this path but too stubborn to back away from a fight, Edge folded his arms and glared at her. "I'd know."

"You didn't. None of us did," she fired back. "You are our leader, Edge, but that doesn't make you infallible. I know you want to protect all of us, but you *can't*."

Their gazes locked. "I protected you. Didn't I? Every way I could. No matter what the cost. And I'd do the same for everyone else in Haven. Cyborg or not."

That should have ended it. He'd taken beatings to keep her safe. He'd killed for her, and he'd do it again.

Her words were little more than a whisper, but he heard them clearly along with the pain threaded beneath them. "I never asked you to do that. The people you hurt...the ones you killed. You shouldn't have done that for me."

"After what they did to you, you couldn't protect yourself. If I hadn't done it, who would have?" he asked, but his anger was gone. No matter what she thought of him, he never wanted to be the reason she was in pain.

She raised her chin and gave him a look of pure defiance that made his cock twitch with desire. He hadn't seen this side of her until recently, and he liked it, even if he refused to acknowledge his interest in her.

"We're not on Reamus anymore," she said. "I can take care of myself, Edge. You worry about everyone else."

The room was so quiet he could hear his own heartbeat. Everyone was watching this exchange like it was some kind of spectator sport. *Fraxxing* wonderful. Now he was distracting the others from what was important. It was time to end this conversation and get back to what mattered—preparing for the fight coming their way.

"Thanks for clarifying. I'll do that." With that said, he pushed back from the table and reluctantly dragged his focus from River to Tyran. "Now, about opening up the armories. What say we put it to a vote?"

3

LEAVING the council room after the meeting took longer than she'd expected. Everyone wanted a chance to wish her good luck and thank her for all she'd done while she'd been part of the council. The only one who didn't approach her was Edge. He had left mere seconds after the meeting was adjourned, which was probably for the best. The two of them couldn't seem to be in the same space for more than a few minutes without things getting heated between them. It had been that way since they'd come to Haven, and at times she missed the way it had been before they'd come here.

River tried to push the thought aside, but it lingered even after she said her final good-byes and headed home.

Before. Her time at Reamus had been a never-ending nightmare, but she and Edge had managed to survive, in part, by leaning on each other. He had protected her as best he could, and she had been the only one who could reach him when he fell into his darkest and most dangerous moods. He'd kept the other males away from her because he knew her programming made it impossible for her to deny any request for sex. He'd done what he could to keep the guards away from all the cyborg females, too. Not that any of them dared to touch River. They knew she was the personal project of one of the head researchers and kept their distance.

A shiver danced down her spine and left her feeling cold despite the afternoon sunshine. She tried not to think about *him*. The man who had rewritten her entire personality and made her into someone else. Someone she didn't recognize. Even before they'd come to Haven, she'd worked hard to undo the behavior modifications and programming that was forced on her. She would never be who she'd been before the changes, but she wasn't that person, either. She was someone new, and that would have to be enough.

A message came through one of her internal channels. She didn't feel like talking, but she checked the sender's ID in case it was important. It was Phaedra, and the message was brief, not needing an answer.

"If you need anything, let me know. Change is a wonderful thing, but it's also scary as hell. I'm here if you want to talk or just eat chocolate mousse and hide from a certain grumpy cyborg we both know. By the way, he came back after you left. I think he wanted to say good-bye and good luck to you. That male needs a swift kick in the thrusters...but we both knew that already. Anyway, I wanted you to know he was looking for you. Do with that information what you will."

River snorted softly. The last person she wanted to deal with right now was Edge. He'd been an important part of her life once, but that time was over. They weren't imprisoned any longer, and she wasn't the same person. Their friendship, if that's what it was, had been a product of their situation. There'd never been anything romantic about their bond, despite her secret wish that he saw her as something more than a victim to be protected. He never had, and given the way he'd spoken to her today, he never would.

Just one more thing she needed to put firmly in her past. Tomorrow was a new day, the first one in her life where she'd be free to do whatever she wanted.

Instead of walking straight home, River opted to take a stroll through the city. She wanted to see for herself how everyone was dealing with the bombshell news that they'd been infiltrated by the Shadows. Everyone at the meeting had reported their observations, but she'd been focused on setting up the system and then scanning the cyborgs to clear them from any suspicion. Her part in that was done for now, another task she could let the others finish. Even if it would be hard for her to relinquish the chance to check herself for corrupted code, or anything else that might indicate she'd been compromised. Again.

The first thing she noticed on her walk were the empty sidewalks. It was a warm, clear afternoon, but there weren't as many beings out and about as there should be. Shopkeepers stood at their doorways, chatting to each other as they waited for customers. Some of the food vendors appeared to have packed up early, leaving street corners empty.

The citizens of Haven were persevering, but she

could sense the unease that permeated every part of the city. Everyone seemed to be staying close to home, and those few beings she saw walked with brisk purpose, as if it wasn't safe to be outside.

They couldn't continue this way. As much as it pained her to admit it, Edge was right. They needed to do more than simply wait for the next blow to fall. The fact she could actually think of going on the offensive without a sense of dread told her how much of her old self she'd recovered since being freed. She'd never again be the fearless soldier the corporations had originally programmed her to be, but she no longer lived with constant anxiety, either. It felt like she had finally found the balance point between the two states.

Her stroll took her past the space port. Unlike the rest of the city, the port was still a hub of activity. Cargo shuttles came and went, transferring goods between the surface and orbital platform where most trade vessels were required to offload. For security reasons, only a few of the smaller vessels were permitted to land at the port directly. Their captains were all carefully vetted and their crews had to undergo medical scans before being allowed to leave their ships.

Another lesson the colony had learned the hard way after a visiting ship had brought a common virus with them and infected nearly all the Vardarians.

River stopped near the fence to watch for a while. Like every other cyborg on the planet, she was not permitted to leave, though the council had pushed that restriction to allow them access to the orbital station and the shipyards now operating in orbit around Liberty.

She'd taken several trips to the platform in the past year as part of her leadership duties. If her plans worked out, she'd be making many more.

She had recently applied for flight training, and her acceptance letter had come only a few days ago. As preparation for the application, she'd accompanied one of the pilots on their daily flights to the platform. Thrash had been a surprisingly patient teacher, and his encouragement had helped her decide to try for a career as a pilot.

She had other options, too, but none of them offered the sense of freedom that came with flying. Up there, she was only responsible for herself. After giving up so much of herself to help others, she couldn't think of anything she wanted more.

The sun was low in the sky by the time she returned home. She lived near the bridge that spanned the Sterling River. From her kitchen window she could see the water swirling by, and she'd even had a swing built so she could sit out on her deck and take in the view. Tomorrow morning, she intended to start a new tradition and have her breakfast outside so she could enjoy the morning light on the water.

Instead of a proper meal, she indulged herself with a double-thick chocolate milkshake. On a whim, she sent an image of the decadent beverage to Skye with the message, *"Here's proof that I'm taking care of myself."*

Skye replied, *"Where's the whipped cream?"*

"Good question," River said aloud as she returned to the food dispenser and requested the addition, with a dollop of chocolate sauce for good measure.

"Oversight corrected," she sent back to Skye.

Drink in hand, she went upstairs to continue her night of indulgence with a hot bath. "Sissy, run the bathwater at my usual temperature and add some bubble bath. Raspberry this time."

She'd named the household AI system Sissy. After all she and the others had been through, it didn't feel right to treat anything with a voice like it was an unfeeling tool, even if that's what it actually *was*.

The scent of raspberries reached her before she even made it to the top of the stairs. She took in a deep breath and let it out slowly. Another breath, and the tension in her shoulders eased. This was her space, a place no one else had ever been, not even her friends. In the early months, it was the only place she felt truly safe. Later, it had become a sanctuary of a different kind, a private place where she could reflect and recover from the past.

Milkshake still in hand, she toed off her shoes and let her bare feet sink into the thick rugs that covered most of the floor. Brightly colored, the vivid patterns should have clashed with each other but somehow didn't. The rugs had been one of the first things she'd bought for herself—a declaration of independence and a rebellion against the dreary backdrop of industrial gray and black she'd been surrounded by for most of her life.

This space was different. The walls were a buttery yellow, though that was hard to see through the collection of paintings and sketches that covered most of them. Some were little more than rough outlines, but others were complete works. More canvases sat on the floor or leaned against any available surface, and several of them had been torn or broken as if slashed or struck.

When one of her counselors had suggested art as a way to process her feelings, she was certain they hadn't intended for her to destroy the works as part of her process. It worked for her, though.

River sipped at her milkshake as she moved to stand in front of her most recent work. After a moment, she reached out to brush her fingers over the faces captured on the canvas. One by one, she recited their names. Torrent. Pulse. Quake. Ebony. Slate. Her batch-siblings. They had all died in the Resource Wars, but she still missed them. Capturing their likeness helped her hold on to their memories in a way that revisiting her data files couldn't.

This painting showed seven figures, but only those five had faces. The other two... She took a deep quaff of her drink, but the whipped cream and sugar couldn't cover the bitter taste that filled her mouth. The other two figures were also her batch-siblings, but she'd never been able to complete a painting that captured all of them together on one canvas. Hunter and Chase had survived the wars, but they were as lost to her as the others. Every memory she had of them was tainted by the knowledge of what they'd done.

They'd been freed together and made plans to find a place they could live in peace. It was all they wanted, and despite her anger, she hoped they'd manage to find it for themselves. When the squad of masked and armored mercenaries had burst through the door of their room, she'd been the only one home. In the fight that ensued, she'd managed to send her brothers a message warning them not to come home.

They'd responded with promises that they'd find her and get her back. That they wouldn't leave her alone... but they had. She'd never heard from them again. They hadn't come for her. She would have known if they'd tried. She was sure of that. They'd given up on finding her and left her to suffer. She could never forgive them for that.

"No," she said the word aloud. "Tonight isn't about the past. It's about the future. My future."

She raised the drink in a toast to herself and took another sip. "Sissy, play some music, please. Something from my relaxation list."

"Files acquired. Playing now."

The opening notes of a Vardarian opera score filled the air. It was one of her favorite pieces and always put her in a good mood.

Then the music abruptly ended as a voice out of her nightmares spoke. "Hello, Petal."

The milkshake she'd been enjoying fell from nerveless fingers, the chilled concoction splashing over her bare feet. It matched the sudden wash of icy black fear that crashed over her, leaving her screaming soundlessly in denial of what she heard.

The voice—*his* voice—continued speaking. "I've missed you so much. If I could have taken you with me, I would have. I never wanted to leave you alone. I tried... but you know that. You were there at the end. You know I didn't want to go without you, but they wouldn't allow it. You saw them force me away. It wasn't my fault,

Petal. I need you to understand that. *They* did this to us."

She fought back the gut-tearing panic to reclaim some semblance of awareness. Reality returned to her in jagged flashes. She was alone. The bastard wasn't here. But he knew where she was. Panic threatened to overwhelm her again at the thought. He'd found her.

No. No. No. How?

"I have good news, though, Petal. The ones that made me leave you aren't in charge anymore. There's a new order now, and they are very interested in my research. I've told them all about you. They want to meet you and see for themselves how wonderful you are. You and I will be together again. Soon, Petal. I promise."

The music came back, but she didn't hear it. All she heard were his last words repeating over and over inside her head. "Together again. Soon."

She came back to herself with a throat-tearing scream, her fists beating against the sodden rug beneath her. She kneeled in the remains of her milkshake, her legs parted and head bowed in a posture of subservience that had once been part of her daily existence. She'd sworn she would never kneel like that again, but here she was. All it took was the sound of his voice to reactivate the programming she'd fought so hard to break free of.

Tears of anger poured down her cheeks as she stood, shaking with emotions she couldn't name. The need to vomit was almost too strong to ignore. Memories of the last time she'd seen him flooded her mind, taking her back to Reamus Station. He'd ordered her to come with him, and she'd been too weak to fight the compulsion to obey.

The guards were there, stun batons out as they tried to force the other cyborgs into cryo-pods. Edge had been there, fighting with the others. They'd killed as many as they could, somehow sensing this was their chance. In her memory, the coppery tang of blood and screams of pain surrounded her, but she didn't hesitate. She had to follow him. Her master. Doctor Troyan Jens.

Beyond the prison area was a different kind of chaos. Beings jostled each other through tightly packed corridors. She caught fragments of conversations as Jens wove his way through the crowd.

The station was compromised.

Everyone needed to evacuate.

Take nothing with you. No room.

The part of her still free of Jens' control tried to make sense of things. The cryo-pods. They must be trying to take at least some of their creations with them. But Edge, Striker, and the others were resisting. Did that mean they'd be left behind? What would happen to them?

Angry voices sounded ahead of her. Dr. Jens shouted at someone, "She comes with me!"

"No, sir. My orders are clear. No unrestrained cyborgs may to be brought on board. If she's not in a cryo-pod, she's not coming."

"She *is* restrained! She obeys me without question! Petal is the result of years of experimentation, and my work cannot continue without her."

She'd watched as Jens had argued, his pitch and volume rising as his gestures grew wilder with each of the guard's refusals.

He'd shrieked in protest when two more guards

dragged him aboard one of the ships. As he vanished, she'd felt a tiny kernel of hope kindle in her breast. She had no idea what would happen in the next few hours, but nothing could be as bad as what she had already endured. At the worst, she'd die. But at least she'd die free.

"I will never go back," River whispered as she wiped the tears from her cheeks with angry swipes of her fingers. "I'm not your Petal anymore. My name is River."

The declaration clarified things for her, and she felt an unexpected sense of calm. "My name is River," she said again, louder this time.

Then she smiled. It was brittle and raw, but it was still a smile. "And I'm not going to be here when you come for me. I won't endanger my home or my friends. Not this time."

With that said, she turned toward the closet and the stash of supplies she'd placed there in the days after she'd learned about the code that could have turned her against everyone she cared about. She'd hoped this day would never come, but she'd prepared for it anyway.

Whatever future she'd hoped to find in Haven, it wasn't going to happen.

It was time to go.

4

THERE WERE things she had to do before she left. The first was to double-check the contents of the bug-out bag she'd packed. It wasn't as if anyone could have come in and messed with it, but her time as a soldier had taught her that it was better to be sure you had everything before heading out. Where she was going, every item mattered.

The inventory list in her onboard files matched the one neatly printed and tucked into the top of the bag. One by one, she removed the items, compared them to the list, and set them down on the bed. Once everything was accounted for, she repacked the bag and set it by her bedroom door with a comm unit set neatly on top. She'd need that soon.

The scent of raspberries wafted by her, reminding her of the bath she'd been about to take. She had no time for that now, but she still needed to wash the remains of her milkshake off her legs and feet.

She stripped off her soiled clothes and tossed them into the laundry chute out of habit. She wouldn't be here when they were returned—clean, dry, and folded—in a few hours.

Then she hurried to the bathroom and took a hasty bath, rinsing herself off with handfuls of water. It wasn't the long soak she'd wanted, but it would have to do.

Once she was back in her room, she dressed in dark, loose-fitting clothing and then dragged a large container out from the back of her closet. She set it down on the floor, searching for a moment until she found the scanning pad located off to one side. She pressed her thumb to the pad and waited. A soft beep was followed by a *snick* as it unlocked.

Once opened, the lid of the case revealed a small army's worth of weaponry and ammunition. The lower part of the case contained a full set of combat armor. She'd had it custom made when she was still on Astek Station, what felt like a lifetime ago.

No one in Haven knew about her private stash except for Phaedra. After the negotiations were done and the cyborgs were assured of their place in the new colony, Phaedra had taken River shopping. It took several days to visit the various shops and dealers recommended to them by the cyborgs who ran the Nova Club. They'd helped her with some of the purchases, and Phaedra had paid for the rest. Being a princess had advantages, including access to the royal treasury of the Vardarian empire.

Thoughts of her time on Astek Station gave her an unexpected pang. The station where she'd taken her first steps toward a life of real freedom had been destroyed some time ago. The Gray Men had murdered so many innocents in their attempts to maintain control over the sector, but in the end, most of them had lost everything anyway.

Too bad it wasn't *all* of them. If that were the case, she'd be able to stay in Haven. Too many had escaped, though. Including the man who featured in the worst of her nightmares.

Astek's replacement, Defiance Station, would be finished soon, but she wouldn't be around to hear about it or find out what came next for everyone involved. She had to leave. It was the only way to keep Haven safe.

She couldn't wander around Haven outfitted for war, so once she confirmed everything was accounted for, River closed the case and set it beside her bug-out bag. Then she turned and looked around her room one last time.

"Damn you for doing this to me. And double damn you for violating the only place I truly felt safe," she muttered.

The last thing she did was to retrieve a data stick from a desk drawer. She moved to place it on her bed but then paused. She needed to do something else. Without giving herself time to overthink things, she tapped a button on the side of the device and recorded a brief message. It would be automatically added to the end of the message already stored on the data stick. Once she was done, she set it down in the center of the bed where whoever came looking for her would find it.

River turned her back on the bed, her room, and everything she'd created here. She gathered up both the bag and case and carried them downstairs. Then she set the last part of her plan in motion.

The comm unit she'd prepped for this eventuality was as heavily encrypted as she could make it and would never be used again. What she planned to do next would violate the rules that governed the cyborgs on Liberty, and she didn't want to get anyone in trouble for helping her.

Once she sent the message, there'd be no turning back. River gave herself a moment to review the situation. She had to be sure this was the right move. It took less than a second for her to be certain. This wasn't just the right thing to do. It was the *only* thing she could do.

"Sissy, engage security protocol Exodus Omega."

"Executing," the AI said.

Once she was sure there would be no record of what happened next, she activated the comm. "Vixen. Vixen. Vixen. The Dove is in flight. Repeat, Dove is in flight. Are you available for capture?"

It was the one potential hitch in her carefully orchestrated plan. She couldn't be sure if the intended recipient of the message was even in the system at the moment. If she wasn't, River would switch to her secondary plan.

She was still pulling on her favorite set of combat boots when a reply came through. Text only.

"This is Vixen. Message received. Fox will capture and bring Dove to the nest."

River curled her lip at that bit of news. Vixen was near enough to receive the message but not close enough to make the pickup. That meant involving yet another being in her plans. She had hoped to get away without dragging anyone else into this mess, but needs must and all that. If Hezza B. trusted Thrash to do this, she would, too. Besides, it wasn't like he ever knew the contents of the cargo he sometimes delivered to and from Hezza's ship. This would be no different, except this time, the cargo would be a cyborg.

5

____

"What do you mean she's gone? Gone *where*?" Edge forced the words out through gritted teeth. He stared at Skye, anger making his nerves sizzle.

The Bar None was usually a bustling place at any time of day, but right now it was as silent as the void. A group of cyborgs gathered around the table where he'd been enjoying a late lunch. He hadn't known anything was wrong until Skye and the others had trooped inside wearing matching expressions that told him a shitstorm of trouble was about to land in his lap.

Skye shrugged. "We don't know. There's no sign of forced entry. The residential AI indicates she returned home yesterday evening and made herself a milkshake. That matches the message she sent me around the same time. She wanted me to know she was taking care of herself. That's the last time anyone heard from her."

"What about after that? The AI should have noted when she left," Edge asked, frustrated that he'd been left out of the loop for this long. If they'd told him right away, he could have tracked her down by now. She was his responsibility, dammit.

"Less than an hour after that, the system locked itself down. Phaedra and her team are looking at it now. Phaedra said it looked like River ordered the shutdown herself."

"Of course she did," he growled, more to himself than anyone else. "Why make it easy for us to find her and get her out of whatever trouble she's in?"

"She might have done that." Skye held up a data stick. "But we don't know because the data stick she left for us to find is bio-locked. So far, none of us can open it."

Edge held out his hand, and Skye passed the device to him with a knowing smirk. "Think you'll have better luck?"

He pressed his thumb to the scanner. The little device chirped twice and then the red band around the scanner turned green.

Before he could comment, Skye laughed. "Imagine that. She left the message for you."

He raised a brow and gave her his best cold stare. "I'm her leader. Of course she'd want me to see this first."

When Skye seemed ready to say more, he slashed the air between them with the flat of his hand. "Now is not the time for jokes. We need answers."

He touched a small button on the side of the data stick. At first he wasn't sure what form the information would take. A map? Text? A recording of some kind?

When an audio recording started, he had his answer. River's soft voice filled the air. "Hello, everyone with Edge right now. I know this will sound cliché, but if you're listening to this message, I'm already gone."

Where? He thought. *Where* the *fraxx* are you?

"If you check the shuttle logs at the spaceport, you'll find one of them recently took an off-the-books flight. I flew it to the northern continent, well into the polar area, and had it return on autopilot."

She laughed softly, though he didn't like the sadness in her voice.

"I've scrubbed the coordinates, so don't bother looking. Though I know Edge will insist it be done, anyway."

"Damn right I will." He pointed toward Striker and his human female. "Find that shuttle and go through everything. Take someone from Phaedra's team with you."

"On it," Striker said, already moving for the door.

River's message continued, "I left because I had to. I'm a threat to everyone who matters to me, and this is the only way I can protect you all. I've known this day might come since we discovered what the bastards on Reamus did to me. I wanted to stay and be part of this wonderful place, but it wasn't meant to be. If I'm gone, something happened that made it clear I'm a threat to Haven. I made contingency plans, and now I'm implementing them."

Edge grimaced and snarled wordlessly. She should have come to him. Why the *fraxx* would she think she had to do this alone?

Another soft laugh rose from the device in his hand, this one entwined with layers of regret he heard beneath the levity. He knew that sound because he lived with it every day, and it pissed him off to hear it in *her* voice. He was their leader. Her leader. It was his job to shoulder the burden of what might have been for the others.

"Stop making that face, Edge. I know you want me to get to the point of this message so you can order everyone to go looking for me, even though that's the last thing you should do. Let me protect all of you the best way I know how. Let me go."

The recording paused. There was a click, and then the playback began again. This time her voice was different, more uncertain than he'd heard from her in ages.

"I'm adding this so you all know why I had to leave. Dr. Troyan Jens sent me a message today. You'll find it attached to a music file. Sissy will know which one." River's voice cracked, but she kept talking. "He found me, and he has the means to get a message to me despite all our security. You all know what that means. He wants me back, and I will not put anyone else in danger because of one man's insane obsession. I need to be somewhere else, somewhere far from the colony. If I am, it's possible he'll leave the rest of you alone.

"Protect each other. Protect our home. Don't let them tear down everything we've built together. I wish I could be part of that, but you have to let me go. It's the only way."

That seemed to be the end of the recording, but before the device shut down, he heard two words whispered so softly he almost missed them. "I'm sorry."

Hearing that was a sucker punch to the gut. He

woofed out a breath he hoped no one else heard as he fought back a wave of emotion he had no interest in dealing with. Feelings were a luxury a male like him couldn't afford. They'd slow him down and make him weak when the situation demanded he be strong.

No one noticed his moment of weakness, though. They were too busy having their own reactions to what they'd heard. Some were horrified. Others were angry. Most were uneasy even speaking that son-of-a-starbeast's name.

"Why would this doctor guy come after River and not anyone else?" Edge looked around to find the owner of the voice. It wasn't one of his cyborgs. It was... "What are you doing here?" he demanded, scowling at Cameron Allen. The human male had no reason to be part of this discussion.

The male threw up his hands and grinned. "Hey, don't snap at me, big guy. I was minding my own business, enjoying my meal, when all of you showed up and started talking."

Edge rubbed a hand over his bearded jaw and tried not to grind his teeth in frustration. Right. They were in the middle of a public restaurant, and that was no place for the conversation that needed to happen next.

He stood up so fast several of the cyborgs nearest him backed up as if expecting violence. "I need to speak to the rest of the council. The rest of you do what you can to help the investigation. Talk to Skye. Make a plan. I want regular updates."

"So, we're going after her?" Skye asked. "Despite the fact she told us not to?"

"We are. Which is why I'm going to update the council. They'll need to help, and we need to prepare for whatever is coming."

"You mean Jens," Skye said, her voice flat and cold.

"I do. If you haven't told that spymaster of yours who he is and what he's capable of, now's the time."

"He knows," was all Skye said.

"Then he'll understand what's at stake." Edge clapped a hand on Skye's shoulder and squeezed briefly. "I know this isn't easy for you. River wasn't the only one he hurt. If you need to talk…"

Skye barked out a laugh. "You may be my friend, Edge, but you are the last one I'd come to if I needed to talk about my feelings. You're more screwed up than the rest of us combined."

He flicked up two fingers in a rude gesture he'd learned from the Vardarians and strode toward the door. "Anya, I'll be back to pay up later. Gotta go."

"I'll add it to your tab," the human female retorted.

"Hey, why does he get to run a tab?" Ruin asked.

"Because he pays his. You don't."

"That was one time!"

Despite everything, Edge left the tavern with a ghost of a smile on his lips. An interrupted meal, a new crisis, and someone getting called out for their bullshit. It was a typical day in Haven.

Everyone came as soon as he sent out the call. Some arrived at their usual meeting place ahead of him, and the rest hurried in within minutes. There were no friendly greetings this time. Everyone took their seat and waited in silence for the last few beings to arrive.

The moment they were all seated, Edge told them everything he knew. It wasn't much, and to his annoyance, it appeared that at least one other council member already knew River was missing. The prince didn't say anything, but his expression made it clear he wasn't hearing anything new.

The questions came at him fast and furious the moment he finished his summary of the situation. With River gone, he was the only cyborg on the council. An election for several new seats, as well as hers, was scheduled for the beginning of next month, but for now, he was the only one present who knew what had made her decide to leave.

After a few frustrating minutes of cross-talk and repeated questions, he raised both hands to get everyone's attention. "You need to understand that none of us talk much about our time at Reamus Station. Not even to each other. You haven't been left out of the conversation, and we weren't withholding information deliberately. But revisiting those memories isn't something any cyborg is eager to do."

"That's understandable," Denz said. "But now, we need to know more. Are you willing to fill us in?"

Edge appreciated that the Torski phrased it as a question and not a demand. "I'm the only one who can."

He lowered his hands to the table and steepled his fingers. "Multiple experiments and research projects were going on at any given time. Some of them didn't directly involve us, but most did. In some ways, it was a shared nightmare, but in others, our experiences differed."

He tried to thread the needle between what the others needed to know and what would be deeply intimate secrets that weren't his to tell. As far as he knew, he was the only one River had ever talked to about what Dr. Jens was trying to accomplish and what he'd done to her.

"River was one of the ones whose experience was unique. All of you know that three cyborg females were created with specific behaviors encoded into their programming and reinforced with behavior modifications. Skye, Talia, and River."

Everyone nodded.

"What you don't know is that others were in the program. Those three were the only ones who didn't suffer mental deterioration so severe they were deemed as failures and terminated."

Edge let his words hang in the air for several seconds as the others took in what he meant. They all knew the cyborgs had endured mental and physical degradation and abuse, but he needed to remind them all of how bad it had really been. Every month at least one of their number had been terminated or had found a way to escape their eternal hell through suicide by guard.

"How many were there?" Zanyr asked.

"Eight females were created using variations of the same process. One was captured after the war and added to the program. Dr. Jens believed it was possible to alter our core personalities and turn us into what they'd wanted us to be from the beginning—compliant, battle-ready weapons of war with no free will."

"Those *fraxxing* bastards," Raze growled. "Did it work?"

Edge cocked his head from side to side. "Yes and no." He looked at Denz. "Do you remember what River was like when you first met her at Astek Station?"

Denz's eyes narrowed as he caught on. "River was the one they recaptured?"

"She was. Can you tell the others what she was like back then?"

Denz nodded and looked thoughtful for a second before speaking again. "She was soft-spoken, almost meek. It took incredible courage for her to speak up at all. She had so much compassion and was determined to do her best to represent the cyborgs from Reamus Station, despite how hard it was for her to face her fear. And she was afraid. I remember that."

"I didn't know that," Zanyr said. "That doesn't sound like the female I met when I arrived here."

"She's worked incredibly hard to reverse what Jens did to her. The female I knew, the one Denz described, didn't call herself River. That was the name she chose for herself at some point during the war. I have no idea what her name was before that. But when I first met her, Jens had given her a new name. Petal."

"River was a soldier? I would have never guessed," Raze said. The veteran warrior looked nonplussed at the idea. "She's so...gentle."

"Everything I know, I learned from River while we were all captives. I suspect her kindness and compassion were always there. It might be why Jens selected her for his experiment in the first place. We have no way to know. What I do know is that River fought in the Resource Wars for several years. She was released with the majority of the cyborgs but then recaptured at some point. She was already at Reamus by the time I arrived, and by then, Jens had already started adjusting her personality."

He scrubbed at the back of his neck, reluctant to share the last details he knew. This wasn't his story to tell, but it was important the others knew.

Finally, Raze broke the silence. "What else did he do to her? There's something you haven't told us."

"I'm not sure we need to know," Tyran said.

"And I am sure I don't want to know, but we need to." Denz glanced around the room before meeting Edge's gaze. "Don't we?"

"You do. But this is not something anyone else needs to know. She kept this a secret, even from the other cyborgs." Edge cleared his throat. "Jens wasn't satisfied with merely turning River into an obedient soldier. He decided to make her into something else, too. A pleasure slave. The more obsessed he became with her, the more he tried to change her core personality to match his twisted fantasies."

Every being present reacted with various combinations of shock and horror.

"And we're sure he's the one who sent the message she mentioned?" Zanyr asked and then raised his hands to fend off Edge's glare. "I'm not saying she's lying, but we need facts, not conjecture."

"I've got people retrieving the message from her household AI right now. I or any other cyborg who had contact with that bastard Jens can do a voice analysis and confirm it's him, but I have no doubts. River wouldn't have left if she wasn't sure of the threat. She *wanted* to be here."

It wasn't fair that she'd been forced to leave the colony she'd helped to establish. Not every cyborg was entirely happy to be trapped on this world, but River had made a home for herself here. She deserved that... and once again, he'd failed to keep her safe.

Fraxx.

6

<hr>

IF RIVER HAD HER WAY, she would never have seen the inside of another cryo-pod. It was one more reason to hate Jens and the cabal he worked for.

The hardest part was always the wait between when awareness returned and the point at which she had enough muscle function to press the button that opened the pod. She hated lying in the dark, her limbs still too weak to move. It was like sitting in a nightmare version of death's waiting room, unsure if you would return to life or die here, cold and alone.

The second she could move, she pressed her palm to the switch that would let her out. The door swung up and away, and suddenly she was bathed in warmth and light.

"So much better."

"Go slow. If you're anything like me, you want out of the damned coffin, but if you try it before you're ready, you'll just face-plant on the floor. That's a problem because you're too heavy for me to lift." A human female with short-cropped gray hair grinned down at her. "Must be that fancy metal plating they put on your bones."

"Must be." River cracked a smile. "Nice to see you, Hezza."

"Drink this." Hezza handed her a bottle of water. "It's good to see you too. I gotta say, though, I'd hoped we'd never have to go through with this plan of yours."

"You and me both." River popped the tab on the bottle and guzzled most of the contents before talking again. "Thanks for the water. And for everything."

"You paid me to take care of you. That's what I'm doing. Implying anything else would be bad for my reputation." Hezza pointed a thin finger at her. "So don't tell anyone I'm being nice." With that, she produced a steaming mug of what had to be *ja'kreesh* from somewhere behind her. "Bottoms up. Once your brain is working again, I want to know what happened to make you fly the coop. I knew at some point one of you would want me to smuggle them off-planet, but I never figured it would be you. Now that big, broody one. Edge? He would have been my bet. He'd head off to find a war somewhere so he could lose himself. I know the type."

River drained the last of the water before switching her attention to the gloriously large mug of liquid many referred to as Torski rocket fuel. It had enough natural stimulants to keep one of the massive aliens on their feet for a day or more, and had become the drink of choice for many of the cyborgs once they discovered it.

She sipped the drink slowly, eventually easing herself out of the cryo-pod and onto a nearby bench.

"You're set up for this," River commented.

"Let's say this is not the first time my cargo arrived in a cryo-pod. Not a nice way to travel, but it sure makes it easy to hide undocumented life signs in my cargo bay if I happen to be scanned by the authorities."

"Did that happen?" River asked.

"Yeah, but it wasn't anything out of the ordinary. I made a few stops on my usual run before making the detour to that little slice of hell you chose as your new home."

River waved off the comment. "The nicer the planet, the more likely someone will show up and try to colonize it or claim it for resource processing. The place I picked has already been surveyed and rejected. The environment is too harsh for a colony and it has insufficient resources for any corporation to want to strip mine it."

Hezza snorted. "It's a *fraxxing* dust bowl. That's why no one wants to live there. But I get your reasons. What I want to know is why you're here? I thought this plan was a last resort, all-hope-is-lost scenario."

"It was." River took her time before she spoke again. This wasn't the first time she'd been in Hezza's ship. Thrash had brought her on board several times, with the freighter pilot's permission, to let her get comfortable with the layout of the controls and even run a few of the ship's basic flight sims. Hezza had offered advice and encouragement, and she'd even given her the full run of the ship.

"This kind of work isn't for everyone," Hezza had told her. "There's freedom, sure, but you won't feel that when you've been cooped up inside your ship for three weeks. If this is going to be your world, you better be sure you can live with that."

It was good advice. She would have liked being a pilot. Even if it was just ferrying cargo from the surface to the orbital platform and back. That wasn't in the cards for her, though. Not anymore. She'd likely leave the dusty rock she'd chosen to hide on after a decade or so, but to do that, she'd need a ride, and Hezza wouldn't be flying forever.

That was a problem for another time. One that would be a long while coming.

"So? What's the story?" Hezza prodded.

River told her more than she'd originally intended, and when she finished, Hezza leaned in and gave her a hard, heartfelt hug. "No one should ever have to deal with the shit you've seen. You do what you need to. But if you change your mind, or the fecal matter hits the intake fan, you better promise me you'll call for help. I've been on my own for a long time, and I know better than most how hard it can be, even when it's what you need to do. There are times, my girl, when you need friends."

River patted Hezza's arm. "I will."

"Mmhmm." Hezza gave her a knowing look. "You'd better. And to be sure I hear it when that day comes, I'll leave a relay buoy in orbit. I've got the perfect doohickey for the job, too—something small and stealthy enough not to draw attention. It can relay any message you send, and you can be sure I'll receive it. Not quickly, mind you, but eventually."

River wrapped the older human in a warm hug of her own. "Thank you. If you ever find out Jens is dead? You let me know. Maybe he'll get hit by a comet and I can come home."

Hezza laughed. "From your lips to the ears of whatever entity created this mad universe."

Saying the word *home* triggered a cascade of thoughts and feelings. Haven was the first real home she'd ever known, and leaving it left an empty place in her heart. By her sense of time, she'd only been away for a matter of minutes, but the feeling of loss was still there. "I wonder how they reacted to the message I left. They must have found it by now."

Hezza snorted. "They aren't taking it well. Whatever you said, it was like dropping a cannister of rocket fuel into a blast furnace." She spread her fingers wide. "Kaboom."

"*Veth.* That wasn't my intention. They have enough to deal with already."

"Intentions are funny that way. Doesn't matter what you meant, once you sent the message, what happened next was out of your hands. I've heard from my girl Anya, Striker, and even the pretty pink princess herself. They told me what happened, that you were gone, and that they were scouring the planet for you with no luck."

River winced. She'd hoped they'd be too busy to do that right away. The longer it took for them to start looking, the more time it would take for them to realize she wasn't where she said she was.

Hezza's tone softened. "Did you really think they wouldn't try to find you? You've got good people who care an awful lot about you back there."

"I know. But I asked them not to."

Laugher rang out, bouncing off the bare walls of the cargo bay. "I imagine they considered that option... for about ten *fraxxing* seconds."

She huffed out a rueful breath. "Fair point. Did they say anything else?"

"They did. Every one of them asked me to keep an eye and an ear open for even the tiniest scrap of a rumor about you or any cyborg female seen traveling alone. I think they suspect you've left the planet, but they don't want to say too much."

"Because if they do, word will get back to Unified Governments and the corporations that another one of the scary, dangerous cyborgs from Reamus Station is roaming the galaxy unsupervised."

"Because Chance has done so many terrible things since she escaped." Hezza rolled her eyes. "And she's hardly unsupervised. Erik is as protective and growly as a newly mated Vardarian."

"I wonder if she foresaw my departure." It hadn't occurred to River that the only other cyborg to leave Haven could have known what she would do. Chance's abilities were unique. Instead of a combat role, she'd been designed to aggregate data and calculate outcomes based on what she'd analyzed. That made her one of the most dangerous cyborgs in existence, and now she worked with Nova Force and others to help track down criminals, including the Gray Men and now the Shadows.

"If she did, she wouldn't have said anything. She's careful about what information she gives out. You know that."

"I do." River finished the last of her *ja'kreesh*. "If you

see her again, tell her I'm glad she found what she needed to be happy."

"Will do. And I'll see her soon. I'm scheduled to run some supplies to Defiance Station, and she's already there along with her husband and the rest of the Nova Club crew."

"That's good to hear. I always hoped I'd get to see the new station someday. Chance did predict that the cyborgs would eventually be allowed to leave Haven." River shrugged. "Plans change."

"Indeed, they do. That's something I had to drum into my daughter's head when she was growing up. She wanted consistency, the kind of stable home-life she saw some other kids have. It wasn't something I could give her, though. I'm glad she's found it now. And she proved something I'd always suspected in the process."

"What's that?"

"She's such a handful it takes two beings to keep her out of trouble. I never had a chance. But now she's got Tra'var and Damos watching over her, she's in good hands."

River laughed. "Yes, she is. Though I suspect any tendency to find trouble comes from her mother."

"She certainly thinks so. She demanded to know if I'd smuggled in anything for you, like gear to help you survive in a 'hostile environment.'" Hezza made air quotes around the last two words. "I could honestly say that I had not since everything I did for you was delivered to a different star system per a standard contract, and it was all legally paid for."

"And the only thing you actually smuggled for me was, well, *me*. And I was an outbound package."

"Exactly." Hezza winked at her. "Any reason why they thought you'd need to survive in a hostile environment?"

"I told them I was heading to the planet's polar region. I even sent a shuttle there on autopilot as a decoy."

"Uh-huh. Gave them a false trail to follow to give yourself some leeway before they worked out you weren't there?"

"That was the plan. If there are still spies among the citizens of Haven, news of my departure will make it to Jens or someone else in his organization, eventually. If it keeps him away from the colony, that's a win."

It was the best she could do, but a little voice in the back of her mind whispered it wouldn't be enough. Jens had already proven he would not stop looking for her. His obsession could only end one way. Either he died, or she did, and she didn't intend to be the one cashing out.

7

———

Two HOURS of combat drills and sparring hadn't done much to improve Edge's mood. He would have gone for another round, but he'd already faced off against most of the others present. The ones left were all too young or inexperienced to go up against him. The last thing he wanted was to seriously injure someone because he wasn't at the top of his mental game.

He might be a killer, but he still refused to do harm to anyone who wasn't his enemy. That hadn't always been possible while they'd been imprisoned. The guards had forced them to fight each other. Sometimes to test their abilities and others, he suspected, purely for the assholes' entertainment.

Now that he could make his own choices, he preferred to use violence only as a last resort. The practice arenas, this one in particular, were one of his favorite places in the colony. Day or night, at least a few beings were always working on their technique or just blowing off some steam. This was one of the few places he could go to avoid feeling alone without having to be sociable. Comradery was offered without judgment.

As a result, he'd learned several new fighting styles. Some of the moves were more theoretical than practical, given his lack of wings, but knowing them ensured he'd be prepared against a winged enemy. Not that he expected war with the Vardarians. They had a warrior ethos he could appreciate, even if he didn't understand some of the nuances of their culture.

He wasn't a nuance kind of male. Never had been, never would be.

He grabbed a towel from a nearby shelf and wiped the sweat from his face. He'd done all he could for his state of mind. Maybe now he was calm enough to get some serious thinking done and figure out where the *fraxx* River had disappeared to.

When she'd thrown down her challenge that she could take care of herself, he hadn't really believed it. Now he did. River wasn't the same female he'd known on Reamus. That cyborg had lived in a constant state of anxiety and an all-consuming compulsion to please others.

The plan she'd put together had been bold, clever, and done right under their *vething* noses. He was *definitely* not pleased with her right now, but he wasn't happy with himself, either. He hadn't truly seen how much she'd changed. He'd sworn to be there for her, to protect her...and he'd failed to do that. Again.

"Where did you go, you little minx?" he muttered to himself. Edge was almost certain she wasn't anywhere on Liberty anymore. They'd scoured the planet and found no trace of her. The human government would be thrilled when they learned that tidbit of information. For now, they were continuing on the assumption she hadn't broken the rules, but all of them suspected she'd done exactly that.

He walked around the edge of the sand-covered floor of the arena, keeping a respectful distance from any sparring matches in progress. Partway there, he spotted three familiar figures. Wreckage and Ruin came into Haven more often since finding their mate, but they still weren't a common sight around the practice arena unless it was practice day for the rangers. The male cyborg with them was one he saw far more often. Thrash. He was one of the ones being considered for a council position and had sat in on several meetings. The male was brash and occasionally thoughtless, though he had settled down somewhat in the last few months.

When Ruin spotted him, he nodded and turned in his direction. All three of them wore grim expressions, but Thrash looked like he was considering an emergency extraction for himself. Reinforcing that impression was the way Ruin kept one hand firmly clamped on the younger cyborg's shoulder.

Wreckage spoke over their internal channel. *"Got a second? Thrash has some news I think you need to hear."*

The tone of Wreckage's message made Edge think it wouldn't be good news, but at this point, he'd take what he could get. It's not like the rest of them had made any progress.

"Walk with me," he said and gestured toward one of the communal rooms each arena had. Each location was

more than a place to train. They were community hubs with large-scale kitchens, meeting rooms, and the capacity to become whatever was needed—from emergency shelters to celebration halls and even large-scale medical clinics.

They crossed the sand-covered floor, met up, and continued to walk the rest of the way together. They all kept a wary eye overhead, aware that the Vardarians fought as many aerial battles as ground-based ones. That led to the potential for both weapons and combatants hitting the ground without warning.

Once inside the relatively spartan room, Ruin closed the door and took up a guard position inside. That confirmed it. Whatever Thrash was about to say wasn't good. Edge waited for someone to speak up, but the silence stretched on until what little calm he'd managed to reclaim during his workout evaporated. "Spill it."

Thrash leaned against the side of one of the tables stacked around the walls. "It's about River. I mean, I think so, but I can't be sure." Thrash never sounded uncertain, even when he was wrong. Edge didn't have time for the other cyborg to waffle his way through an explanation.

Edge squared his shoulders, locked eyes with Thrash, and activated a subprogram he rarely used. "Sit-rep. Now, soldier."

Thrash might never have been in combat, but he'd been programmed to respond to anyone coded as a senior officer. He snapped to attention, his next words coming without hesitation.

"Yes, sir. The night River vanished, I was working.

Nothing out of the ordinary, just bringing cargo to the orbital platform. I got a request from an inbound freighter pilot to bring up a crate that wasn't on my manifest. This isn't uncommon, but it's not exactly procedure."

"Uh-huh." Thrash had held a few jobs around the colony, but he seemed to have settled into his most recent job of flying cargo shuttles up to the orbital platform. "We'll discuss how often you and the others break the security protocols that protect this place at another time. Why do you think this has anything to do with River's disappearance?"

"The timing, sir. I mean, Edge." Thrash shook his head and relaxed his stance a little. "And the cargo wasn't typical. Usually, last-minute additions are small items. This was a large metal crate, totally locked down. It was a heavy bitch, too. Big enough I burned some extra fuel getting off the planet."

"How large?" Edge made a note to find out how often these "last-minute, small items" were being smuggled on and off planet, but that was an issue for another time.

"Two meters long and about a meter-and-a-half high." Thrash demonstrated the dimensions by holding out his hands.

"What do you think was inside?" Edge pressed.

"I don't know. But it was big enough for someone to hide in. I mean, that's not likely, because all cargo is scanned for that kind of thing before it's allowed into the warehouse, but..."

"And you only now thought to say anything?" Edge was ready to tear his hair out. Or possibly kick Thrash's ass from here to the nearest asteroid belt.

"I ran into some mechanical issues and had to stay on the plat for a few days. I got back a few hours ago. I'd heard some gossip that someone was missing from the colony, but no details. As soon as I learned the rest of the story, I talked to these two. They hauled me over here to tell you what I knew." Thrash gave Ruin and Wreckage a baleful look. "I could have told him all this over a voice channel and saved us some time."

Edge was about to ask for more information, but something about Thrash's continuing discomfort set off alarm bells. Why wouldn't he want to tell him everything in person? The answer was obvious. Because there was something Thrash didn't want to admit, especially if he was within striking distance.

"What aren't you telling me?" he didn't bother hiding his growing irritation.

Wreckage and Ruin both looked at their companion with dawning comprehension. "You *fraxxing* idiot. What have you gotten yourself involved in?" Wreckage demanded.

"Nothing!" Thrash raised both hands. "Nothing serious. I just..." He deflated with a long sigh. "Sometimes I run cargo that's not on the manifest. Nothing dangerous!" he added hastily. "This is my home, too. I'm not going to do anything to endanger us. My contact buys hard-to-find items from the local shops and then has me deliver them so she—uh, so *they* can resell it to folks who don't have the same access to Vardarian goods."

"So someone who has permission to land here and leave their ship to shop in the colony has been skirting the rules about exporting goods?" He didn't have to guess who that would be. "How long has Hezza B. been doing this?"

To his credit, Thrash didn't try to deny anything. "I have no idea. I got involved a couple of months ago, and like I said, it's never anything dangerous. Hezza would never endanger her own daughter."

Ruin chuckled softly. "And Anya would kill her if she did anything that stupid."

"So, you delivered this mysterious crate to Hezza?" Edge prompted him for more information.

"I did."

Edge spun on his heel and walked toward the door, gesturing Ruin to get out of his way. "We'll table the rest of this conversation for another time. I need to track down a certain freight jockey and find out where the hell she took our wayward citizen."

And once he found said citizen, he was going to spank River's ass red. The thought popped into his head, complete with a visual that had his cock surging to life. *Not. Now.*

And not ever, he added the afterthought out of habit. Every time he thought about River that way, he shut it down immediately. She deserved so much better than someone like him.

The thought gave him pause. He'd told himself that since the beginning, and maybe back then it was true. But now? When it came to River, he couldn't be certain about anything. He'd been wrong too many times already.

He contacted several cyborgs at the space port and the orbital platform, instructing them to track down

Hezza B. and put him in contact with her as soon as possible. One advantage to living in a Vardarian colony was access to their tech. The aliens' communication abilities were far better than what even the human military used. Once they found the freighter pilot, he'd be able to converse with her in something close to real time, despite the differences in their comm systems.

While he waited, he accessed the flight plan the female had filed before departing. River was either still on board or had gotten off somewhere along the way. Finally, he had a place to start looking.

She might have told him she could take care of herself, but that didn't mean she had to be alone. "I'm coming, River," he murmured as he made his way through the nearly empty streets and back to his residence. "Whether you want my help or not."

8

RIVER'S CHOICE of hiding places was the result of a number of factors, including proximity to Hezza's usual routes. The system she'd finally selected was only a short jump—less than two days—and was in an area of space without much traffic. The deviation shouldn't be noticed, and Hezza had a cover story about a malfunctioning nav set to go if anyone asked questions.

"Last chance to change your mind," Hezza said over the ship's speakers.

River didn't bother answering. They both knew this was the way it had to be.

"Okay then. Welcome to your new home in the ass-end of beyond. Which is what I've designated this system as, by the way."

"You're crap at naming things," River called out as she rapped her knuckles against a nearby bulkhead. "No one sane would ever call their ship the *Desperate Gambit*."

"Never said I was sane," Hezza replied, her snappy

comeback almost covering the concern in her voice. "And if we're going down that path, I will happily point out that I'm not the one about to ride a dropship from high orbit to the surface of a planet rated so inhospitable to life that even the corporations want no part of it."

And that was another reason she'd picked this place. No one would come here by accident. Anyone who showed up could safely be considered a threat. She intended to treat them as such.

When what little she'd brought with her was stashed inside the dropship, River took a few minutes to freshen up before meeting Hezza back on the cargo deck.

"I am not thrilled about this plan of yours," the older female stated.

"Honestly, it's not my favorite idea, either. It's just the only one I have. When I set all this up, I thought it would be to keep me from acting against my friends. I always expected *I'd* be the enemy that had to be dealt with."

"You got what you need to handle that bastard doctor if he shows his face on Dust Bowl?"

River snorted at the nickname Hezza had given the planet they orbited. "I do. And I'll have time to make new plans once I get down there. I'm a cyborg. I can handle anything that place can throw at me. If Jens shows up, he'll have more than a pissed off cyborg trying to kill him. The whole planet will be in on my side."

"I still don't like it." Hezza reached out to touch her arm gently. "You don't have to do this alone. I could go back and get a few of your friends..."

River raised her hands to stop Hezza from saying

anymore. "It's bad enough I left the colony. If more of the cyborgs leave, there will be repercussions. I don't know what else they could do to us, and I don't want to find out." She took Hezza's hand and squeezed it. "I'm worried about you. The best thing you can do now is to forget I was ever aboard the *Gambit*."

"I've spent my whole life avoiding trouble. I've become an expert at avoiding blame and side-stepping unpleasant things like prison time. After you're gone, I'll send the bots to do a bio-scrub of the interior. There won't be a scrap of your DNA left for anyone to find."

"If you're questioned, how will you explain the cryopod?"

"I've already got a buyer lined up for it. I kept it in a warehouse on Liberty because I knew no one there would steal it. Can't say that about many other places on my usual route." Hezza winked. "I told you. This is what I do. I'll be fine. And when I hear anything you need to know, I'll find a way to get the information to you."

"Thank you. I'm grateful for everything you've done for me." She gave the human a quick hug and then danced away before Hezza could protest.

"I fulfilled the requests of a paying client. A very generous client. Nothing more."

Hezza jerked her chin in the direction of the dropship. "Hang on tight on the way down. It'll be a bumpy ride."

"I will." River climbed into the claustrophobically cramped space inside and strapped herself in. With one last wave, she closed the hatch and prepared for the drop. Something thumped against the hull behind her, and then a deep vibration thrummed through her seat as the dropship was clamped into place and pushed toward the cargo ramp at the back of Hezza's ship. Red lights flashed on her console, indicating the cargo bay was venting atmosphere.

More lights flashed as the ramp opened, and she briefly wished she had a view-port so she could watch what happened next. The dropship had a basic AI that handled everything from departure to landing. All she could do was hang on and hope. If it all went to plan, in a few hours she'd be setting up camp near the rest of the items she'd paid Hezza to drop here over the last few months.

"It had to be this way," she whispered as the dropship started its descent. Even as she spoke the words, a tiny part of her refused to agree. She couldn't listen to that part. Her heart didn't know what was best for her. If it did, it wouldn't still be asking why she'd walked away from the one male she'd ever wanted... and could never have. Edge had never seen her that way.

The dropship's AI managed a near perfect landing. She stepped out of the cramped cockpit to see she was only a few dozen meters from the scattered collection of crates and containers that held everything she needed to survive. Some of it was scavenged from the gear the IAF had donated for the cyborgs' use when they had first arrived at the colony. They'd sent over enough nutri-bars, dry rations, and surplus military items like cots and camping gear to fill several warehouses. No one had missed the bits and pieces she'd acquired for herself. She wasn't the only one to do so, either.

The rangers had taken a good portion of the camping gear to outfit themselves for patrols. After all, it had been intended for them to use. Those doing the donating just never envisioned the cyborgs would be welcomed as full members of the colony. They thought River and the others would live their lives on the outskirts of Haven, making do with second-hand gear and the generosity of their alien caretakers.

She snorted. Like she would have agreed to the deal if that was the case.

Dragging everything to her chosen location and setting up her camp felt unexpectedly nostalgic—the feel of canvas beneath her hands, the familiar scents that wafted up from inside each crate as she opened them. Some of the memories made her sad. Others made her smile. Without even being aware, she fell into a rhythm honed over the years she'd been in combat.

Even the landscape felt right, like she'd been here before in that long ago life. The sky overhead was a paler blue than the one she'd known, but her research told her that the frequent dust storms and thicker atmosphere would create breathtaking vistas at sunrise and sunset. Those same dust storms were why she had to set things up as quickly as possible. The weather on this planet was as hostile as everything else, and the winds could reach speeds that could flay the flesh from her bones if she was caught without shelter.

She hadn't only brought military surplus, though.

Some of it was of Vardarian make, purchased from local shop keepers and artisans. Obtaining it and then getting it here had cost her every favor she'd earned and almost all the scrip she'd received as compensation for the pain and suffering she'd endured during both her times as a slave.

The surveys and data she'd used to find this place had come from Sevda. Well, technically, they'd come from the AI of her ship. As a former corporate scout, Sevda had mapped dozens of systems over the years, including the entire area of space around what was now Liberty. Hearing about how she'd met Raze and the way they'd bonded and decided to forge a future together was a tale she'd fought to include in the official record of how the colony had come to be.

Sevda had taught her how to read the charts and extrapolate information from what was little more than raw data.

Thinking about Sevda gave River a pang. She missed her, and even her grumpy husband, Raze. The thought put her at the top of a slippery slope that would only lead to feelings she had no time for. First, she had to get herself sorted and settled. She'd have time to deal with the ramifications of what she'd done later. Long nights alone with nothing but her thoughts to keep her company would give her plenty of time for regrets and remorse.

The surveys Sevda had provided were how she'd found the spot she intended to make her permanent camp. Outcroppings of red and orange rock dominated the area, and some of them formed a natural enclosure with a narrow gap as the only way in or out. The enclosed area was sandy, with a small pool of clear water at one end. Scrubby brush and small, fibrous trees twisted into strange shapes by the wind huddled near the only source of water.

The rocks offered more shade than the trees did, so she placed her shelter next to a massive boulder with enough of an overhang to provide some shade during the hottest parts of the day.

The shelter itself was one of the most expensive items she'd had Hezza deliver. It could be hermetically sealed to keep out the sand, dust, and wind, and while it was almost as cramped as the dropship cockpit, it contained everything she'd need to survive here for the long term. It had a water reclamation system on par with one from a starship, a simple cooktop, and a loft that functioned as both her general living space and sleeping area.

The batteries it used for power were housed in a separate section near the back and could be recharged using solar panels or a wind turbine. Given the amount of dust in the air, cleaning the panels would be a daily chore —one of many she'd have to take on.

The second building she put up was a combo workshop and storage tent. This was a far simpler structure with canvas walls and an internal framework that took her far too long to set up. She'd done this dozens of times in her life but never on her own. She took it as a reminder from the universe that she'd need to remember that going forward. One person could do everything that needed doing, but it would take her longer and require some resourceful thinking to accomplish it all.

"I can do this," she said aloud, her words carried off by a hot and arid wind.

It was still a few hours before sunset, but something told her she'd need to be inside her new shelter before then. A quick glance at the sky confirmed her suspicions. The sunlight had dimmed slightly as it was filtered through a reddish haze. With no weather satellites or other equipment, she would have to rely on her instincts when it came to predicting storms. This meant she could never stray too far from camp, which was fine. Everything she needed was right here. The rocks gave her shelter, the pool of clear water was maintained by an underground spring, and all her supplies had survived their descent and were ready to use.

She dragged the last of the crates inside her new workshop and storage area and took a few minutes to double-check that the bolts and ropes she'd used to secure the tent were all in good order. It would take days for her to complete the preliminary setup of her camp, but for today, she'd done enough.

The whisper of sand blowing across the rocks blended with the first mournful moans of the wind as it blew into the crack and crevices of her new home. She still had a few minutes, and she wanted to see the coming storm for herself.

She picked out a likely vantage point and made for it, making leaps that no human could have managed. With a little work, she could make the ascent even easier by leveling some of the more obvious landing spots. She grinned as she reached the top of the outcrop. One more task to add to her ever-growing list.

One look around her confirmed that the view was worth the effort. In fact, this would serve as a perfect lookout point. From here, she had a clear view of the entire area. She was above and behind her camp, allowing her to see anyone or anything that approached the only entrance to her newly established home. The sky ahead of her was relatively clear, but when she turned to look behind her, she spotted the storm. A wall of shifting darkness spanned the horizon, boiling across the landscape and consuming everything in its path. "*Veth.* That's a little nastier than I was hoping for my first storm. I guess everything is about to get stress tested in a serious way."

She scanned the horizon again, using her onboard enhancements to estimate the height and general size of the storm bearing down on her. If it was more or less circular, it would take hours to pass. She had no way to know that and wished yet again that she could have put some micro-satellites in orbit to help her with things like understanding the weather and spotting potential incursions. Anything in orbit would only attract attention, though, and the risk of being discovered outweighed anything else.

Once she'd seen enough, she made her way back down to her shelter and went inside.

She felt like she should say something momentous to mark the occasion, but nothing came to mind. She'd done all she could to safeguard the others and escape Dr. Jens' ongoing obsession with her.

That would have to be enough.

9

———

EDGE DESPISED FEELING HELPLESS, and he liked waiting for something to happen even less. Currently, he was experiencing both of these feelings, and it was making him more than a little crazy.

He paced the deck of the little ship he'd managed to obtain for this mission. It had almost no firepower and was smaller than he'd like, but it was *fast*—faster than any of the shuttles he would have been forced to steal if Sevda hadn't agreed to lend him her ship. Once he'd told her what River had done with the scans and reports she'd given her, it was an easy ask. Sevda hadn't known what River was planning, and she was horrified that she'd inadvertently helped the stubborn little minx.

"Eddi, anything new to report?" he asked the ship's AI.

"I would like to report that I have a very demanding passenger who persists in stomping on my deck and asking questions he already knows the answers to." Eddi's voice was clear and soothing, with a slight inflection that made it sound female.

Edge grinned a little at the AI's sass. "Do you talk to Sevda that way?"

"Of course. I have an adaptive learning algorithm and Pilot Sevda was with me for many years. Aspects of my personality are a reflection of hers."

"So, she infected you with sarcasm and sass?" The former corporate scout was a force of nature, which made her a good match for Raze, not to mention one of the few humans he trusted completely. She'd been the driving force behind getting Liberty declared a colony just so Raze could continue living there, and later she'd made every cyborg feel welcome.

"To quote my former pilot, if you spend enough time flying solo in the void, even an argument with an AI with attitude issues is better than another hour of silence."

"Sarcasm aside, how long until we finish this last jump? I'm going stir crazy."

"Thirty-one hours and eighteen minutes. Then we'll need to transit the remaining distance to the planet using normal engines. Unfortunately, this means you have another thirty-seven hours before you can leave this vessel. Apologies."

"It's not your fault. You've made this run faster than any other ship I know."

The AI chirped softly. "I was not apologizing to you. I was offering my condolences to my deck plates."

He had to fight the urge to flip off the AI. If his temper was so ragged he was ready to hurl insults at a machine intelligence, there was only one thing to do—hit the tiny fitness area and try to burn off some of his frustration on the treadmill. It was that or take a spacewalk, and that was not a smart thing to do while the jump engines were bending space-time.

It was a walk of about five paces to reach the ladder that led to the lower deck and the tiny recreation area. How the *fraxx* had Sevda stayed sane all those years? She'd managed to survive out in the black with no one but her ship to talk to and less space than most prisoners were entitled to.

"Going below to run for a bit. Let me know if anything changes."

"Of course."

He got two-thirds of the way to the lower deck when Eddi spoke again. "Passenger Edge. You have an incoming message. Make that two messages. Would you like to view them?"

He really didn't. He already knew what the gist of each message would be. What did he think he was doing? Where was he going? And who the *fraxx* did he think he was, taking off without telling anyone.

He climbed the ladder and made his way to the cockpit before replying. He didn't want to hear the messages, but if he didn't, they'd keep trying until he gave in and answered.

"Play whichever one is marked with the highest priority first," he instructed Eddi.

"They are both marked at the highest priority setting. However, one of them is tagged with the heading, 'View me first.' I assume you'd like me to play that one?"

"Yeah." He could already guess who had sent that

one. Sure enough, Denz's face appeared on the viewscreen, a scowl etched deeply into the big male's features.

"I'd ask where the hell you think you're going, but I don't imagine you're going to give me that information. I was going to demand you turn around and get back to Liberty before the IAF discovers we're now missing two *fraxxing* cyborgs, but that ship left orbit about ten minutes ago. The Interstellar Armed Forces knows you're gone. So wherever you are, don't let them find you before you finish whatever you think you can accomplish out there on your own. I'm starting to wonder if you and River don't share some of the same programming. Both of you are determined to do things solo."

Denz sighed. "But there's nothing any of us can do about that now. You made your choice, and as *fraxxing* pissed off as I am about it, I also understand why you did it. Maybe better than you do, since you seem to be clueless about certain things the rest of us see clearly."

The big male raised a hand. "Lecture over. Now to the important stuff. The military is looking for you. Nova Force has been brought in—Team Three, to be exact— which means they're less likely to shoot on sight since they've been to Haven and know we're not the enemy. Not even you."

"You should be aware that Hezza is on their shit list, too, so if you're in contact with her, tell her to stay away from Haven. Anya mentioned her mother is allergic to authority, prison food, and handcuffs, so she won't enjoy the reception she gets if she shows up here any time soon. I'm assuming she was the one who got River off the planet, which means she's got a lot to answer for once this galactic shitstorm blows over."

Denz leaned closer to the screen, his gaze intensifying. "Find River. Fast. We're working on contingencies to get both of you somewhere safe, though none of us are sure what that looks like right now. Once she's with you, let us know but don't use standard comms. I've been informed that Eddi will know how to get a message to us. Not that the AI should be obeying you, since you apparently *stole* Sevda's ship."

Denz's all-black eyes glittered with amusement. "Because of course that's what happened. At least, that's what the Interstellar Armed Forces was told, so they have designated you as a dangerous fugitive in possession of stolen property."

Edge winced. *Fraxx.* Could this situation get any more complicated?

"Take care of yourself. Find our runaway and get back here. We're okay for now, but I don't expect the Shadows or Torex to miss an opportunity to make our lives more difficult. Denz. Out."

The next message was from Prince Tyran. The Vardarian repeated all the same warnings and requests but with more polish and less swearing than Denz.

Nothing in either message needed a reply. "Is Denz right? Can you get a message back to them without it being intercepted?"

"I can. Sevda made several improvements to my systems after Haven was founded. She believed a time would come when it would be needed. I did not understand at the time, but I now have more data and believe I comprehend her intention."

Edge stretched and started to rise from his seat. "And now for that workout."

"Another message arrived while you were viewing the other two. It's audio only. Do you wish for me to play it before you leave?"

"Who is this one from?" he asked as he sank back into the copilot's chair.

"Unknown. All identifiers have been scrubbed. I have scanned it for malware and other threats and found nothing of concern. I should also note that it is tagged with two words."

"What's the tag?"

"Hey, asshole."

"Ah." He smirked to himself. "That would be from Hezza. Play the message."

It was audio only. "Hey, asshole. I take it you're the reason I've got to hightail it out of this part of the galaxy for the foreseeable future? I know you wouldn't give me up directly, but someone smarter than either of us must have put the pieces together after our last chat. Thanks for that.

"I'm sending this message to Haven in hopes that some benevolent soul will forward it to you. I'm betting you've already gone after her. If not, you're an even bigger fool than I thought you were."

A pause was followed by a wry snort. "I've got Nova Force sending me repeated requests that I come in to answer some questions. They're more polite than I'm used to, but I'm still going to decline the invite. Don't worry about me. Not that you would. You're focused on one thing right now, and you better do right by her. She's hurting, and I think *you* are part of her problem. You and that Jens jerk. If you get a chance, punch him once for me. Then slap yourself upside the head for letting whatever the hell happened between you two get in the way of what needs to happen next. If you need me to explain what that is, you should turn around and go back to Haven. She doesn't need your protection, you big idiot. She needs *you*."

Another pause. "And, yes, I'm drunk. I do that when I have the law chasing me. It's a tradition. That's all I had to say. Good luck. Kill the asshole. Kiss the girl. Don't get those last two mixed up. Trust me when I say it leads to complications you don't need."

That was the end of the message. Considering how badly their last conversation had gone, he'd expected more insults and general cursing. Hell, he was surprised Hezza had reached out at all. He'd laid into her with unrestrained fury and frustration when they'd finally made contact. They'd both had a lot to say, and most of it hadn't been relevant. Still, she had given him River's location...eventually.

He grudgingly added Hezza to the short list of humans he trusted. He might have even put her on the much shorter list of humans he *liked*, but she was the one who had taken River away from him... so no.

"Now for that workout," he said as he got to his feet. He was already on the treadmill before he noticed his mood had already improved. An unfamiliar sense of calm had taken hold. He ran anyway. It would help pass the time. Besides, he thought better while he was in motion. Something about the message had helped him to relax, and he pondered what that would be. It wasn't the news they'd shared since nothing he'd learned had been good. It must be that two trusted friends had reached out to him at all, sharing what they knew and supporting him, even after he left them behind.

Friends? Edge let the word roll around in his mind. When the *fraxx* had he made friends with non-cyborgs? For that matter, when had he dropped his guard enough to make friends at all?

Still working through that revelation, another train of thought slammed into him at full speed. If those messages were from friends, Denz and maybe even Hezza had offered him some pointed advice.

"She doesn't need your protection, you big idiot. She needs you."

The treadmill's motor could barely keep up as he accelerated into a flat-out sprint. He had a *lot* of thinking to do.

10

THE FIRST FEW days on the planet she now thought of as
DB-1—which sounded better than calling the place Dust
Bowl—passed in a blur of hard work and temperatures
that gave her unexpected insight into what it must be like
to be a blade in a blacksmith's forge. Her enhancements
and medi-bots allowed her to function in the heat, but it
wasn't comfortable. She regretted not bringing along
some of the light fabric dresses the Vardarian females
favored. They'd suit her current situation better than the
military fatigues she'd taken from the stores back on
Haven. By the end of her second day, she'd taken a knife
to several pairs of pants, turning them into shorts. Those
and a tank top were her daily wardrobe, though she kept
wearing her heavy boots. The rocks were surprisingly
sharp, and there were far too many things here that bit
and stung to even think about wandering around
barefoot.

After some thought, River opted to place the solar
panels on top of the rocks surrounding her camp. It took

her longer to clean them that way, but it allowed her to keep the area around her shelter clear of obstacles. It also meant the panels got more sunlight each day. She didn't have concerns about power consumption, but keeping the batteries full meant she wouldn't have to worry if a dust storm or other weather phenomenon blocked out the sun for more than a day or two.

Most of her time and energy were spent making her new home as secure as she could. Motion-activated cameras covered the entrance to her camp and several other areas she considered might be used by someone trying to get the drop on her. She'd had Hezza acquire a few other surprises as well. She slept better now they were all in place.

The cameras did more than watch for intruders. They provided River with her first real look at the local fauna. While the planet had been surveyed extensively from orbit and even had a few probes land on the surface, the information on the wildlife here had been minimal.

There were small invertebrates of all kinds, some winged, some terrestrial. Reptiles were another common sight on the cameras, though she had only seen a handful in person. All the wildlife in the area seemed most active from dusk until dawn. The other thing she noticed was that none of the fauna would stay in one place for long. They moved constantly, keeping to the rocks when they could.

It wasn't until the third night that she spotted the reason creatures here never stopped moving. They were being hunted.

The local predators looked a bit like armor-plated

flounder, only their mouths were on the tops of their bodies instead of the underside. They moved through the sand as easily as a fish through water, ambushing their prey from below and dragging their meals beneath the sand. The ones she'd seen weren't much bigger than a dinner plate, but she had to assume there were larger ones out there where the sand was deeper. Thankfully, these predators, which she dubbed sand sharks, never came too near her camp, probably because of the rocky terrain and shallow sand.

The reason why most of the creatures were nocturnal was obvious. The temperature soared every afternoon, driving most life to seek shelter from the blistering sun. River followed their example. She'd retreat to the comfort of her shelter during the hottest part of the day and pass the time reading on her tablet, watching entertainment vids, and doing maintenance on the gear she relied on to stay alive. The sand and grit got into everything, wearing on moving parts and clogging up the systems that provided her with cool air and safe water.

There was more than enough work to keep her busy every day. Too busy to let herself think about home, or Troyan Jens, or all the people she'd left behind. Nights were a different matter.

The nights were quiet, with only the song of the wind blowing through the rocks and the whisper of shifting sand. Sometimes she'd hear the skitter and patter of individual grains as it blew into the walls of her shelter.

Evenings always brought back thoughts of Haven. She thought about the lush forests and summer breeze that always carried a hint of wildflowers and warm grass.

She missed the bustle of the markets and the scent of freshly baked bread from the bakery on the far side of the river from her house.

To combat the melancholy, River started drawing again. Her small habitat didn't have the room for paints or anything elaborate, but she'd included a collection of sketch pencils and even a few pastels. The simple fabricator she'd purchased could make paper, though she had to be sure to recycle most of it so it didn't take away from other items she'd need.

She sketched scenes from home, like the view of the river from her back porch, along with scenes of day to day that were a composite of memories. She drew her friends' faces, conjuring their likeness as if that could keep the loneliness at bay. Sometimes it did.

Tonight, it wasn't working. She sat at what she jokingly called her kitchen table. It was little more than a fold-down shelf between two narrow benches. When pulled down, it provided a flat surface just big enough for a couple of plates, or several sheets of paper and her art supplies.

She hadn't really been paying attention to what she was doing. It was something to pass the time and let her process what she was feeling in a constructive way. Or that was what her counselor had called it. The sketch was almost finished before she was aware of who she'd drawn.

Edge. Not the way he looked most of the time, but the way she'd seen him some nights when he'd fallen asleep beside her, determined to protect her even while he slept. It hadn't happened often. Edge rarely slept back then. She didn't know if that had changed, but she doubted it.

The image was a side of him not many of the others would recognize. All his sharp edges were softened, his normally hard mouth relaxed, his lips full beneath his beard.

Veth, she missed them all. She hadn't expected it to be this hard. She'd been alone before, and while she'd expected to feel sad, she hadn't expected the sense of loss that matched her grief for her long-dead batch-siblings. More than anyone else, she missed *him*.

"Stupid," she lashed herself with the single word as she crumpled up the sketch and tossed it against the wall of the shelter. It rebounded lightly and fell back onto the tiny table.

Without thinking, she picked it up and smoothed it flat again, letting her fingers caress the lines of his face as she did.

Why him? she wondered as she stared at the portrait. Of all the beings in her life, why was he the one she had the most trouble moving on from?

It might be because they'd never had a chance. One of them was always too busy, or too broken. Edge had his demons, and she had hers. She would never be whole again. Jens had seen to that. Despite all the work she'd done to reclaim her real self and to rebuild who she'd once been, it would never be the same. She was still broken. A dark, secret part of her would always crave the glorious surrender that came with submitting to someone else's desires.

She could hardly even think about that part of

herself. Talking to anyone else about it would never happen. It was too embarrassing, too humiliating to admit that whatever Jens had done to her, she hadn't been able to undo it. She expected to take that secret to her grave, which was the reason she'd never shown interest in any male in the colony. Even if she found someone she thought might accept her damage, she wasn't sure she'd ever trust anyone in the galaxy enough to give them her submission.

If that wasn't broken, she didn't know the meaning of the word.

Frustration pushed her to her feet. "And that's enough of that. No more wallowing. If you can't find something useful to do, River, get your ass to bed."

Talking to herself was a new habit, but one she figured couldn't hurt. It's not like anyone was around to judge her for it. She tidied up a little and then double-checked that everything was locked down for the night. The last thing she did was strip out of her clothes and place them in a bag near the door. Laundry was on tomorrow's chore list. She'd get it done first thing in the morning and lay it all out on the sun-warmed rocks to dry. It wouldn't be the same as having freshly dried towels set out by the household bots of home, but at least she'd have clean clothes.

She ascended the short ladder to her loft but only made it to the second rung when an alarm sounded.

She reacted immediately by stepping off the ladder and letting herself drop back to the floor. She hit the ground and pivoted until she saw her tablet. Along with the books and other forms of entertainment, it was the control hub for the shelter and her security system.

Her fingers flew over the screen, tapping at icons as she brought up the camera feeds. It felt as if it took ages for the images to load. Part of her knew that was because her sense of time was skewed by adrenaline, but the rest of her mind screamed at the perceived delay. She needed to know what was out there. Sure, it was most likely a sand shark large enough to set off the motion detectors, but what if it wasn't?

One by one, the gray-scale images appeared. When she saw what the fourth camera had captured, a fresh dump of adrenaline flooded her system. She zoomed in, ignoring the way her finger trembled slightly. It wasn't much more than a shadow moving through the deep darkness, but it was enough to tell her that her visitor wasn't a sand shark, or any other type of local fauna. Someone was out there, and they were headed straight for her camp.

Instinct drove her reactions. She hadn't fully prepared for this possibility because she hadn't expected anyone to find her this quickly. She'd been planet-side for less than a week! Her mind raced as she donned the bare necessities for what came next. The chest plate of her armor felt cool against her bare skin as she snapped the clasps that locked it into place. She jammed her bare feet into her boots without bothering to tighten the laces. Like her armor, her weapons were stored in a cabinet near the door. She yanked it open and pulled out a pulse rifle. She did the weapon check automatically, confirming it was in safe mode and had a full charge before slinging it over her shoulder.

Time to go.

She turned off the lights before opening the door. It would give her eyes a few extra seconds to adjust as well as stop light-leakage from announcing the location of her shelter.

Outside, the wind was almost cool compared to the vicious heat of the day, but the sand still radiated enough heat that she felt it through the soles of her boots. She switched her vision to the infrared spectrum, allowing her to see in the dark. She turned up all her other senses, too, even taste and smell. She became the hunter once again, falling back on training and programming she hadn't used since the Resource Wars ended.

For now, she couldn't sense the intruder, but she knew which direction they had to come from, which gave her the advantage. The simplest course of action would be to jump onto the roof of her shelter and wait for them to come to her. It was too obvious for her liking, not to mention she'd risk making too much noise when she landed on the roof. Instead, she made her way up to the lookout point she'd discovered on her first day. It would give her the high ground and ensure that whoever was out there couldn't know her exact position.

She made each leap carefully, doing all she could to stay quiet. Despite her best efforts, the soft thud of each landing and the slip of her boots on the thin coating of sand over the rocks made her wince and freeze until she was sure she hadn't been heard.

Once she made it to her chosen position, she scanned

the entire area. Nothing. With the rocks still radiating warmth, there was no point in trying to look for heat signatures. She'd have to wait this out.

In a motion so ingrained she didn't have to think about it, she tugged on the strap of her rifle, bringing it over her shoulder and into her waiting hands. Cloaked in darkness and as ready as she could be, she froze. Cyborgs could hold perfectly still for hours at a time. None of them knew exactly how it worked, but all of them could make a conscious choice to go completely still.

She waited.

The night wind sang, almost obscuring the sound of movement. The slip of boot moving against sand and then a click that seemed as loud as a rifle shot.

A flash of light erupted, accompanied by a brief cry of surprise and pain.

"Got you," she whispered. Now she knew where the intruder was, even if she couldn't see them. The voice was distinctly male, which ended any supposition that it might be Hezza coming back to try and talk her out of staying here.

The pressure plate she'd buried beneath the sand was wired to a small battery. It didn't have enough juice to be lethal, but it would put any being smaller than a Torski on their ass and possibly knock them unconscious.

She crept closer to the intruder's location, her rifle raised to low ready as she scanned the area. She could have looked through the scope, but while that would improve her visual acuity by a small measure, it would also restrict her field of view. It wasn't worth the risk.

Below her, something moved. Damn. He was back on

his feet already? Did her trap fail? Or was her shadowy visitor not human?

She raised her pulse rifle to the high-ready position. Now he'd given away his location, this would escalate fast.

At least, that's what she thought...until her unknown intruder called out.

"Damn it, River! I knew you weren't going to be happy to see me, but I wasn't expecting to get *fraxxing* flash fried."

She froze. Was that... no? It couldn't be. He couldn't have found her already. Only somehow... he had. It took all her concentration to keep her voice steady and even as she spoke his name. "Edge?"

"In the slightly singed flesh." A shadow moved away from the cover of the rocky wall and came to a stop where she could see him. Slowly, letting her see what he was doing, he set a duffle bag at his feet.

River had already compared his voice to the ones in her files and confirmed his identity, but once she saw him move, there could be no doubt. Edge didn't so much walk as prowl into view, his every movement as familiar to her as the back of her own hand.

"Hell of a place you picked to hide out. When Hezza told me she'd dropped you into a dust bowl, I thought she was exaggerating," he called to her.

"Welcome to DB-1. Now, what the *fraxx* are you doing here and how soon can you leave?" She nodded to herself, pleased at the firm tone she'd managed despite her shock at his unexpected arrival and the hurt at knowing Hezza had given up her location so quickly.

"Can we have this conversation somewhere else? I think something just tried to eat my foot."

"Sand shark. That must have been one of the small ones. The big ones could bite you in half." At least, that's what she assumed, but Edge didn't need to know that last bit.

"Wonderful. I did not come all this way to get eaten. Not to mention zapped so hard I think you fried a few circuits."

"We don't have circuits," she retorted. "And if you'd stayed away like I told you to, you wouldn't have anything to complain about."

Despite the distance between them, she distinctly heard him growl before he answered her. "Did you really think I would do that? That I'd sit back and let you face that son-of-a-starbeast alone?"

"No," she admitted. "But I hoped you'd respect my wishes, anyway. I came here to keep Haven and everyone I care about safe."

"And I came here to keep *you* safe."

Edge yelped, pulled a foot off the sand, and then stomped the ground hard. "*Fraxxing* thing took another bite out of my boot!"

"There's no accounting for taste. Stay put. I'll come to you and show you the safe path into camp."

"And if something tries to eat me in the meantime?" he demanded.

"The sand is too shallow for the big ones to come this close. You're more likely to get stung by something venomous. Or you could stumble into another of my traps."

Grinning, River moved the pulse rifle to rest on her back and began the journey back to ground level. She didn't hurry. It wouldn't hurt for Edge to stew for a few extra seconds as he wondered if anything out in the dark was sizing him up as a snack. Not that anything would want more than a taste of the male. He'd be tough as leather and probably bitter, too. She laughed in amusement as she descended.

"So glad you're enjoying yourself at my expense," Edge grumbled. His banter was out of character, and she wondered why he hadn't started cursing her for leaving the moment he'd come within earshot. That was more like the male she knew. This was a version of Edge she'd only seen once or twice and never for more than a brief moment.

She rather liked this side of him. Not that she'd admit it to him.

"You may have noticed that there isn't much in the way of entertainment out here. I've got to get my laughs where I can."

Once she was on the ground, it was a simple enough matter to orient herself to the correct landmarks and then count her steps so she knew when to avoid the traps she'd placed. Both of them could see well enough without an additional light source, but when she got close, Edge drew a small cube out of his pocket and shook it. The resulting amber light was barely bright enough to illuminate the area directly around him.

River walked to the edge of the light but didn't enter it. "Follow me. Step where I step. You know the drill."

The moment she finished speaking, she turned and moved back the way she'd come.

"I do." Edge paused. When she didn't hear him following her, she turned back in his direction. He hadn't moved his feet, but his head was cocked to one side and he wore a grin that softened his features in a way that made her pulse race.

"What?" she asked.

He waved at her with one hand, still grinning. "Interesting choice in combat gear."

"Huh?" She glanced down, confused, and then realized what he meant. She'd only put on the top half of her body armor and her boots. Apart from a pair of panties, she was more or less naked from the waist down. She hadn't had time for her to put the rest on.

It wasn't that she was embarrassed by her quasi-nudity. Modesty was a luxury none of her kind had ever been permitted. She, Edge, and every other survivor of Reamus had seen each other naked countless times.

This, though. This felt different. Her bare legs made her feel vulnerable. Not to bullets, but to something—or more accurately—to *someone*.

He shouldn't have come after her. And she should *not* be happy to see him again.

11

IN THE INTERMINABLY LONG days leading up to his arrival, Edge had imagined what would happen when he found River. A thousand different scenarios had played through his mind, but in none of them had he imagined River greeting him with sarcasm and a smile. The lack of pants was a pleasant surprise, too, as were the lacy black underwear.

He repressed a chuckle and several indecent thoughts about how easy it would be to tear that scrap of lace off her body. That was something else he hadn't expected. Being near her had triggered a fresh onslaught of desires and dark thoughts. *Why?*

He kept enough of his attention on River's feet to ensure he didn't make a wrong step, but the rest of his focus shifted to River herself. He allowed himself a chance to look at her. Not a passing glance but a long, assessing gaze that let him *see* her while she was too distracted to catch him doing it.

At first, he only saw what he expected to, but then he

registered small differences. Her long legs were still as shapely as ever, but they had more muscle tone than he remembered. Most of her upper body was covered by her body armor, which was also a new look for her. More than that, she looked comfortable in the heavy gear, wearing it like it was a second skin. That was how it had felt to him, too, back when he'd worn it every day.

She moved differently, too. With a longer stride, straight back, and a general air of confidence. Gone was the meek female who always gravitated to the shadows and rarely met anyone's eyes. Even her hairstyle had changed. She'd always worn her dark brown hair short and swept back from her face. Now, it fell in tousled waves he wanted to touch.

He crushed that thought like all the others, determined not to let them take root in his mind. Only, he wasn't sure why he was still fighting this. This new, stronger River was so different than the female he'd thought she was.

She carried her rifle with the easy manner of someone accustomed to using weapons—a soldier, a killer, just like him. The traps were another indication he'd been wrong about her. She wasn't hiding away in hopes of avoiding detection. She was prepared to fight for her life on this harsh, kill-or-be-killed world she'd chosen.

The camp itself brought back memories of past campaigns, though he'd never had equipment as nice as what River had. Where the *fraxx* had she found it all? He assumed some of it must have been liberated from the warehouses on Haven, but not all of it. She couldn't have been here long, but it had the feel of a permanent encampment, with everything she needed to survive as long as needed.

The thought made him growl softly as he accepted that River truly meant to stay away from Haven until she thought it was safe. If he hadn't come after her, how long would it have been before he saw her again?

"Welcome to my camp." River opened the door and stepped back, gesturing for him to go in first. The doorframe was low enough he had to duck his head to avoid a crack to his skull, but once he was inside, there was enough room for him to stand comfortably. It took him a moment to find a spot to put his duffle bag because space was tight. He had to move backward a few steps to give River enough room to join him.

"I would have killed a dozen quartermasters to get a hold of a shelter like this during the wars. I like it."

"Back then, we didn't have scrip to spend. Now?" She gestured around her. "Money can buy pretty much anything you can imagine."

Anger slammed into him as understanding dawned. "You spent the compensation the corporations and the IAF gave you? On this?" He flung out a hand, inadvertently smacking his fingers against the wall.

River raised her head to glare at him, her eyes narrowed and jaw tight. "I did. They said it was intended for us to use to improve our lives and our futures. This is my life now, Edge. What else would I use it for?"

He closed the distance between them, crowding her against the door. "How about something on the planet we're not supposed to leave? Do you have any idea of the shitstorm your departure has caused?"

"Says the cyborg who also left Liberty," she shot back. "I did it to protect the colony. What's your excuse?"

"I don't need an excuse." The words were out before he could think them through. As retorts went, it was as weak as a *Jeskyran's* sense of honor.

"Yes, you do. Because if you are here, Haven isn't as well-protected as it could be. Who else is with you? And for that matter, how the *fraxx* did you even get here?"

"I came alone, same as you."

She scowled. "How? You're not a pilot. There's no way you could have gotten here without help."

"Eddi did the flying."

"Eddi." Her dark eyes widened, and there was no missing the hurt that flashed across her features. "So, Hezza told you where to find me, and Sevda gave you her ship so you could chase me down. I guess I misjudged my friends. I thought I could trust them to keep my secrets."

"You've got it wrong. Thrash was the one who figured it out first. He mentioned his suspicions to Wreckage and Ruin, and they had to drag him in to talk to me. Thrash never told me who his partner was in his little side operation, but it was *fraxxing* obvious to me. I tracked down Hezza and bombarded her with every threat I could think of, including losing access to the colony and every other Vardarian trading post on her route. To say she's pissed with me would be an understatement, but she gave me your location, eventually."

"You said you'd ban her from Haven? You don't have that kind of authority."

"She didn't know that."

"So, you blackmailed Hezza into giving up my hiding

place? How did Sevda get involved? Is Raze looking to kill you for speaking harshly to his mate?"

"I went to Sevda because I needed a ship with an AI. She refused unless I told her where I was headed and why. Once she knew that, she realized she'd provided you with a lot of information about this area. She wants a word with you when you get back."

River shook her head sharply. "I'm not going back! I told you before. I can take care of myself."

"You shouldn't have to!" he said, frustration twisting his words into a snarl.

She poked a finger into his chest. "I left everyone behind to keep them safe. If you're here, you're not at home, helping them prepare for whatever comes next. Don't tell me Torex and the Shadows have decided to give up and go away. We both know that's not going to happen."

He caught her hand in his, flattening it against his chest. "We both know that Haven is as safe as we could make it already. You..." He lowered his gaze to lock eyes with her. "You are not safe. Troyan Jens is sick, twisted, and obsessed with his favorite creation. *You.* I'm not going to let him near you again, even if you're too afraid of me to accept my help."

A storm of emotions flowed across her face. Anger and frustration, he recognized, but something else was there, too.

"I am not afraid of you. Not anymore. That was... it wasn't who I really am. It wasn't *me.*" She raised her free hand and slapped her chest, but her eyes shone with unshed tears. "*This* is me, and I am not afraid of you or him. I have to do this. Even if no one else believes I can."

He pushed in closer until their joined hands were pressed between them. Her words broke something inside him, and all his anger died away in an instant. He saw her so clearly right now—the flush of her cheeks, the way her pupils had dilated, even the way her lips parted slightly—and suddenly he saw what everyone else had. *Desire.*

He released her hand and raised his to her shoulder. Slowly, he let his fingers caress the side of her throat, his thumb stroking her jaw.

She gasped softly, but it wasn't in fear. "Say you want this," he told her in a voice gone husky with need.

River trembled but didn't speak.

He shifted his grip, cupping her chin in his hand so she couldn't look away. "Say it."

"I do. Stars help me. I do."

Every enemy he had could have come for him in that instant, and he wouldn't have noticed. If the stars themselves had gone nova, he wouldn't have cared. All he knew, all he wanted, was her.

His lips crashed down on hers, a declaration of the desire he'd denied for so damned long.

"*Finally,*" he murmured against the silken heat of her mouth.

River didn't answer in words, but when she opened her mouth to invite him deeper, he knew she felt the same way.

12

For the first time in her life, River kissed someone because she wanted to. It was a heady feeling made even more intense because it was Edge. His hands were on her face, his muscular thigh pushing between her bare legs. How they'd gotten here, she couldn't say. Nor could she guess what would happen later. For this second, she had him, and she wasn't letting go.

His mouth slanted across hers, his beard rasping against her skin. His tongue slipped past her lips to twine with hers in a decadent dance as she pondered the insanity of what they were doing and the astounding fact that Edge, the man who never asked permission for anything, had waited for her consent.

She might have kept thinking about everything, but he seemed to sense her distraction.

"No thinking," his voice still carried a trace of command, even as he kissed her.

Then he threaded his fingers into her hair, holding her in place as he uttered a low, primal groan that made her clit throb and sent a shiver down her spine. When he kissed her again, every thought vanished in a blast of searing heat that left her aware of nothing but her need.

Her hands moved over his armor, eager to touch the skin beneath. She found the fastenings easily enough, flipping them open with a familiarity that came from doing it for herself a thousand times or more.

She moaned as the armor loosened, allowing her to slip her hand inside. Hot skin over hard muscle, the tang of male sweat blending with his own unique spice and wood-smoke scent.

His hands moved again, smoothing back her hair before slipping down to the fastenings on her armor. Once it was undone, he nipped the side of her neck, his next words muffled against her skin, though there was no missing the tone of command. "Arms over your head. Now."

"Are you asking for my surrender?" The words slipped out before she could stop herself. She'd meant it as a joke, but there was no way to ignore the subtext in the question. Would he see it too? She didn't know if she wanted that or hoped he missed it entirely.

He raised his head to meet her gaze, his ice-blue eyes piercing her down to her soul. "No, minx. I'm not *asking*."

She raised her arms as he instructed and tried to hide the effect of his words. Did he know? Or was this what *he* wanted?

A satisfied smile played over his lips. "Good girl."

She shivered, her entire body responding to his

display of dominance. Only it wasn't a display. This was who he was.

He pulled her armor over her head. Goose bumps chased over her heated skin as the cooler air of the shelter washed over her.

"Now, you undress me." Edge's voice was silk over steel as he raised his arms as best he could, considering the low ceiling.

She freed him of the chest plate and then the bracers that covered his arms. She stacked it on top of hers in the only space available—the benches and small table where she'd been sketching earlier.

When she reached for the clasp on his pants, he shook his head once. "Kneel. Then do it."

She didn't hesitate. Once she was on her knees before him, she glanced up to find him staring at her with unadulterated need. He touched her cheek with callused fingers. "You cannot know how many times I imagined you like this..."

Words failed her. What could she say to that? How long had they been fooling themselves about what they wanted?

Too long, she decided. But that was about to change.

From her new position, it was easier for her to start at his feet and work up, so that's what she did. First, she untied his boots and then removed the greaves that protected his lower legs. Finally, she rose up to reach for his waistband, but she didn't make contact. Not with her hands. River leaned forward to nuzzle the large bulge of his cock visible through the fabric.

Edge hissed in pleasure, his hips snapping forward in

a quick, greedy thrust that let him rub himself against her lips and chin. His strong hand cupped the back of her head, encouraging her to keep going.

She did.

With shaking fingers, she unfastened his belt and then the clasp of his pants. She nuzzled him again as she tugged the fabric lower on his hips before taking his cock in her hand.

"Fraxx," he groaned, drawing out the word. "Suck me off, minx. I want to feel your hot mouth on my cock." He stroked her hair with surprising gentleness. "But if you make me come before I'm inside you, I'll have to punish you. Understand?"

She nodded. "I understand, Commander."

He groaned again as the last word left her lips. She would never call anyone master again, but Edge... he had always been her commander. The title felt right.

She dragged his pants down lower still, one hand cupping the warm weight of his balls as she wrapped her fingers around the base of his cock. She took the tip of him into her mouth first, swirling her tongue over his crown as he rocked and moaned.

"Deeper," he instructed her. "Let me fuck that pretty mouth."

Her clit throbbed in time to her pounding heart as she obeyed his instructions. She flattened her tongue against the underside of his shaft, massaging it. The moan that rose from her throat vibrated across his length as she bobbed her head in a back-and-forth motion that tore another low groan from Edge.

She kept going, learning what he liked and giving it to

him, following his every whispered instruction. She didn't stop until the sound of bending metal filled the air.

When she paused to look around in confusion, she saw what had happened. Edge's fingers were wrapped around part of a countertop, and he'd gripped it so hard he'd twisted the entire structure.

She'd done that to him. The thought accompanied an intoxicating rush of satisfaction and pride. She wasn't the only one who had surrendered part of herself to this moment. Edge, the one who never showed weakness, had let her see how much she affected him.

Her eyes met his, and in the silence, something deeper than words were exchanged. Not a promise, but a hope... and the certainty that whatever this was, one night would never be enough.

He took her by the shoulders, coaxing her to stand. Once she was back on her feet, he drew her in for a long, demanding kiss that left her senses reeling and her lungs burning for air.

"Your turn," he told her and then drew her in close and turned them, swapping their positions despite the lack of space.

River pointed toward the ceiling. "Bedroom is upstairs."

"We're not going anywhere yet, minx. But we are *definitely* going to use that ladder."

Edge was fighting a battle to stay in control, and he was losing. He'd known it was a lost cause the moment she'd asked him about surrender. Something in her eyes when she'd said it, a note of longing, told him he'd been wrong about River yet again.

He walked her backward, heading for the ladder that led to the second floor. The moment she reached it, he pushed in closer, sandwiching her between him and the metal rungs behind her.

"Take hold of the rung above your head. Do not let go."

A spark of defiance flashed in her dark eyes as she looked up at him. "And if I do?"

"You already know the answer to that. Don't you?"

"I think so."

"Say it," he demanded. "Tell me what happens if you don't obey me."

She swallowed hard, her skin darkening as she licked her lips once before answering, "You'll punish me."

"That's right." He was almost purring with satisfaction now. This was what he'd always dreamed of... but he had to test her one last time. He needed to know if she understood what he was and what he wanted to do to her. "I will turn you over my knee and spank you, River. Then I will keep you there and fuck you with my fingers until you come. But only when I decide you can. Your body will be mine. Your pleasure will be mine. Can you give me that?"

"Yes, Commander."

Commander. That word falling from her sweet lips was better than any orgasm he'd ever had.

Edge kissed her softly, cherishing the gift she'd given

him, astounded at her easy acceptance of what he'd shared. "Thank you, minx."

Tears sparkled on her lashes as she kissed him back. "Thank you. I... never. This is not something I thought anyone would understand. Not after..."

A piece of his heart shattered as she spoke. So much doubt and confusion. How long had she needed this?

He already knew the answer. It was part of who she was. Who she'd always been. Just as it was for him. They were made for each other.

"I know." he kissed her again and then moved back so he could look down at her beautiful face. "It was the same for me. I will never hurt you, River. I don't want your pain. I want your pleasure."

She stood on her toes to kiss him even as she raised her arms and took hold of the rung above her head. "I know. And I trust you to know the difference."

He didn't answer her with words. There wasn't any need. Instead, he gave her exactly what he'd promised. Pleasure.

His hands found her breasts, cupping the soft, warm weight as he teased her nipples with his fingers. She moaned, her eyes closing as he increased the pressure. When he took one nipple into his mouth, she shivered and arched against him, but her hands never moved.

"Such a good girl," he whispered as he moved between her breasts, licking and sucking on them until she was breathing hard. "I want to see all of you. Now."

He kissed his way down her body, enjoying the taste of her skin as he moved over her belly and down to where the scrap of black lace hid her pussy from him.

He got on his knees and leaned in until his nose pressed against the fabric and the scent of her arousal filled his lungs.

"Boots off. Tell me if you need help."

"I got it." Her voice was husky and low as she slipped her feet free. He really had gotten the drop on her. She hadn't had time to tie her boots or put on pants before coming out to face what she thought was a potential threat.

He picked up her footwear and tossed it somewhere behind him. They were in his way, and that was not acceptable.

"Do you have more like these?" he asked.

"Some."

"Good. He caught the fabric in both hands and tore, not stopping until it was little more than tatters that fluttered as they fell to the floor.

"Show me," he told her as he stroked the seam of her pussy with his index finger. "Put one foot up on the ladder and let me see you."

River's breath was ragged as she lifted one leg and set her foot on the rung before letting her thighs part so he could see everything.

"This is mine," he told her as he dipped one finger inside her slick lips to stroke her swollen clit. "It's for my fingers, my mouth, and my cock."

"Yes, Commander." He heard a hint of laughter in her voice that made it even sexier. This wasn't what he'd imagined. It was so much better.

Edge leaned back so he could drink in the sight of her. All of her. Naked. Beautiful. His.

He committed the image to memory, letting it imprint not only on his mind but his soul. When he could stand it no longer, he bowed his head and pressed his mouth to her pussy, parting her labia with his fingers as he explored her body with his tongue. Her clit was easy to find, already swollen and ready for his attentions.

An explosive gasp from River told him she liked what he was doing. Her hips rocked against his mouth, a silent plea for more.

He gave her what she needed, sucking on her clit and using his tongue to tease and torment her until she was trembling and breathless. Honey flowed over his tongue as he pleasured her. Only when she was on the brink did he breach her entrance with two fingers, fucking her in time to the flick and suck of his mouth on her clit.

She moaned his name, and he knew she was close.

He leaned his head back to look up at her. She was lost in pleasure, her cheeks flushed, her breasts still pink from the rasp of his beard against the soft skin. His fingers continued their relentless motion, keeping her on the edge.

"Such a good girl. Do you want to come now?"

She nodded, her eyes opening. "Please. Yes."

That should have been enough, but he couldn't resist making her wait a little longer. "Please, what?"

Her smile was brighter than a supernova. "Yes, please. Commander."

He growled softly in approval as he buried his face in her slick folds again. When she reached the apex of pleasure this time, he drew her clit into his mouth and closed his teeth on it with just enough pressure to send her spinning out of control. Her orgasm came on hard, and he rode each wave with her, prolonging her pleasure as long as he could.

She hung from the ladder, her head bowed and chest heaving as he got to his feet. "You are so beautiful."

She smiled but didn't open her eyes. "Now you're trying to sweet talk me so you can get into my pants."

He chuckled as he moved in closer. "Sorry to tell you, minx. But you're not wearing any."

She cracked open one eye. "And whose fault is that?"

"Mine. Definitely. And if I have my way, you will continue to go without clothing whenever possible."

She raised her brows at that. "If I'm going naked, so are you."

"Deal." he kissed her before she could say anything else.

Her answering kiss held heat and promise in equal measure, and he felt the last shreds of his control give way. Without breaking the kiss, he leaned down and caught hold of her raised leg. Slowly, he drew it around his hips, one hand sliding from her knee to her ass as he lifted her into the air.

She wrapped her second leg around him without any coaxing, leaving his cock wedged between the lips of her pussy with her breasts pressed against his chest.

Fraxx yes. He lifted her higher, positioning his cock outside her entrance. She would be tight. He already knew that from the way her inner walls had squeezed his fingers. He'd have to go slow.

At least, that was his intent, but his little minx made the choice for him. She locked her legs around him and then dropped down to drive him inside her in one fluid motion.

His heart stuttered and his mind froze for a moment as the pleasure of being inside her dominated his awareness.

He growled her name as he drove himself even deeper, not stopping until he was balls deep.

"Naughty girl," he admonished her when he could form words again.

She gave him an innocent look. "But I didn't let go of the ladder."

He would have laughed, but that would have taken his focus away from what was important. "You better hang on tight, little minx."

He withdrew from her body and then snapped his hips upward, filling her completely before withdrawing and doing it again and again. He took as much of her weight as he could, keeping her suspended above him as he fucked her hard. The rhythmic joining of their bodies grew faster in tempo, his balls tightening and his cock thickening as he claimed her body with a frenzy he'd never experienced before.

Their breaths mingled as he kissed her, their tongues dancing as her heels dug into the small of his back. It was the best sex of his life, and so much more than sex, too. He didn't have words for what this was. At least, not any words he was ready to consider.

Together they ascended to new heights of pleasure, their hearts racing and skin slicked with sweat as they climbed.

When the end was near, he changed the angle of his

thrusts, letting his cock slide over her clit. "Come for me, minx. I want to feel you come around my cock."

"Yes. Oh stars, yes!" River cried out as she came a few seconds later.

His release hit only seconds later, his hoarse cries filling the cramped shelter as he emptied himself inside her.

When he was spent, he gathered River into his arms. His head curved over hers as she snuggled against his chest. "You can let go of the ladder now, minx," he murmured.

She made a soft, satisfied noise and let her arms fall to her sides.

With nowhere else to go, he walked backward to the door and leaned against it as he held on to River. If he had his way, he'd never let go of her again.

She stirred and made a halfhearted attempt to loosen his hold on her. "You can put me down now."

He tightened his arms and pressed a soft kiss to the top of her hair. "Not yet."

"Okay," she snuggled in closer and pressed a kiss to his chest. "So, does this mean you're not going to take my advice, get back on your ship, and go home?"

He laughed. "There is not a snowball's chance in a supernova that I'm leaving you behind. I wasn't going to do that before...this. But now? I'm not leaving you, River. Not ever again."

The next time she spoke, River's voice was clear. "Never is a big word. You want to pick something less absolute? Maybe agree to leave now and come back after we're sure it's safe for me to come home?"

"No. I meant what I said." He'd never been so sure of anything in his life, and if she thought she could change his mind, he'd happily correct her misconceptions.

"I'm too happy to argue with you right now. Can we rebook this conversation for some time tomorrow?"

"If you argue with me, you know what'll happen. Right?"

She nodded against his chest. "I know. And if you really don't want me to fight you on this? You should probably come up with a better threat."

"I'll work on it." He had no intention of doing any such thing. She was his minx, and that meant they'd argue now and then. What better way to end a fight than with orgasms?

13

―――――

River rolled off of Edge and onto her back. She left one arm stretched across his naked chest as she sprawled across the mattress they now shared. "I'm starting to wonder if you're arguing with me because you think I'm wrong or because you're hoping for make-up sex."

"Maybe it's both." He caught hold of her hand and lifted it to his mouth to press several kisses to her open palm before letting his lips brush over the barcode on her wrist. They all had them. Like their scars, it was a constant reminder of her time as a slave.

"We've been over this so many times in the past few days. This can't go on forever. I need to stay here. You're needed back in Haven. If for no other reason than to return Sevda's ship."

Edge rolled over to face her, his head propped up on his free hand and his body on full display. "You keep saying that, but you haven't given me a reason why you have to stay on this miserable ball of sand and dust."

Not for the first time, River caught herself admiring

the raw, masculine beauty of her lover. He was leaner than some of the cyborgs she knew. Where some of the males were built like walking mountains, Edge was more like a duelist's blade.

With a mental effort, she dragged her attention away from his body and back to their conversation. "That's because you've already made up your mind."

He grunted. "This would be so much easier if I tossed you over my shoulder and hauled your stubborn ass back to the ship."

"Try it."

"Believe me. I'm tempted. What happened to obeying your commander?"

She snorted with laughter. Over the last few days, they'd begun to be comfortable with each other. "In the bedroom, yes. In the real world? I'm still in control. I have to be."

They lapsed into thoughtful silence that somehow never grew awkward. It was another change to the way they interacted. She liked it. She liked almost everything about spending time with Edge, unless they were arguing. Even that had benefits, since nearly every time they fought, they wound up having sex.

Today was no different. They'd spent the morning doing the usual chores around camp and then retreated to the shelter when the afternoon sun grew too strong. They'd argued before they'd even finished lunch and ended up back in bed with their meal still downstairs, half eaten.

Finally, Edge spoke again. "What if we went somewhere else?"

It wasn't the first time the idea had come up, but something about his tone made her hesitate to say no without hearing more. "We could, but where? Cyborgs aren't exactly welcome in most parts of the known galaxy. If we went somewhere populated, it would be like Haven all over again. If Jens comes after me, I'd be putting innocent people at risk."

"The IAF protects plenty of planets and space stations."

She tapped his chest. "The Interstellar Armed Forces are hunting us. Remember? I'd rather live the rest of my life here than in a military prison. And what if they're not the ones that find us? What if it's Corporate Security? Some of the corporations are still aligned with Torex. They'd hand us over in a heartbeat. And even if they didn't, being in corporate custody would make it too easy for Jens or the Shadows to find us."

Her frustration with the situation bled into her next words. "I didn't pick this place on a whim, you know. I considered all the alternatives I had available. This was the best I could come up with."

"I know, minx. But when you made this plan, you didn't have the same resources you do now."

"And what would those be?"

"Me. You have me." He paused. "And my scrip. I haven't spent much of it. Wasn't really a need back home. The Vardarian society might have its own issues, but they know how to take care of each other."

Before River could reply, he spoke again, his tone brighter now. "Wait. What if we went to Vardarian space?"

"I..." she trailed off as she frantically organized her thoughts into something coherent. "Do you think that's possible?"

"I have no idea, but I can ask. Tyran's a *fraxxing* prince of the empire. Surely he can pull some strings?"

"We'd have to talk to him directly. And we still need to bring Eddi back," she mused. This wasn't something she'd considered before, because if she'd told anyone what she had planned, they would have stopped her.

"Sevda could always come get Eddi. She mentioned that she'd love to go off-planet at some point. It can't be easy for her. She was a scout for decades, and then suddenly she's grounded. In some ways, she's as much a prisoner as we are," Edge said.

"You realize that's true of the Vardarians, too? They can leave, sure, but how many have gone back to the empire? Every single one of them left for a reason, and they don't want to go back. Some of them can't."

He nodded. "I know. I didn't see it at first. I was too angry about..." He grunted and managed a partial shrug. "About a lot of things."

"No kidding," River commented, her tone dry.

"And I'm still not over all of it. I don't know if I ever will be. If I get a chance for payback, you know I'm taking it."

"And you think I don't want that?"

His brow furrowed into deep lines as he considered that. "Is that part of the reason you came out here alone? Revenge?"

"Maybe." She hadn't considered that to be a driving

force behind her decision, but she'd been too caught up in the how part of her plan to really think about the *why*.

She didn't feel like going down that particular wormhole right now, so she changed the subject back to their original topic. "You'd really be okay going into exile with me?"

"Minx, in case I haven't made myself clear, I am not going anywhere without you. That said, if you really want to stay here, we're going to need more supplies."

"Hardly. I've got more than enough to keep us going for at least a year. If you like nutri-bars and reconstituted algae broth."

He grimaced. "I do not. And neither do you. I cannot believe that's what you brought to eat!"

"As backup supplies. The ready-to-eat meals aren't so bad."

"Says you. I'm starting to question your taste, minx. They must have broken something while you were still in your maturation tank."

She stuck her tongue out at him before replying. "My tongue works perfectly, as well you should know."

He leered at her. "I'm not so sure. Maybe you should come over here and refresh my memory."

She hadn't finished formulating a good comeback when a triple-chirp broke up their moment of levity.

Edge had to rummage around in their bedding for several seconds before he found the comm unit he used to stay in contact with Eddi. The AI had the ship parked near one of the planet's moons. Because of the way the orbit worked, it wasn't always within range, so they'd arranged a schedule for updates. Now was not one of those times.

All the humor was gone from Edge's voice as he activated the comm. "Eddi, this is Edge. Report."

"Hello, Passenger Edge. This is the situation. Another ship has entered this system. Using passive scans, I have determined it is heading toward the planet you currently inhabit. It is also broadcasting a message on all known channels. It appears to be a recording on a continuous loop."

Dread wrapped icy coils around her guts and squeezed. It shouldn't be possible, but it had to be Troyan Jens. No one else would enter a supposedly uninhabited system and start blasting a recorded message.

He wanted her to know he'd found her.

"Give me all the information you have. Wait. First, confirm they have not detected you," Edge ordered the AI.

"They have not noticed this vessel. I am using one of the planet's satellites to hide this vessel's presence, as I conveyed to you in previous conversations."

"That's good. Don't let them see you."

"I have no intention of allowing that to happen. However, the newly arrived ship will be able to detect *your* encampment soon. That should be your primary concern, Passenger Edge."

"They'll be able to see the camp, sure. But they won't be able to detect us." River gestured around them. "This shelter is designed to deflect most common scanners, and the rocks that surround it should make that even more difficult. Jens won't be able to know if I'm in here or not, and he won't know there are two of us. We can use that."

"Hold that thought, River. Eddi, you still haven't given me a full report. What class of ship is it? Does it have any identifiers?"

Eddi's calm, impassive voice came back immediately. "The transponder it carries shows that it is a privately owned freighter named the *Maggie-May-Dance*. There are anomalies within the data that make it seventy-seven percent likely that the transponder is showing a fake identity. While passive scans are not overly effective at this distance, I can also confirm that while the vessel's appearance has been modified, there is a ninety-two percent chance it is a military vessel of some kind. Likely a corvette class or similar."

Fraxx. Corvettes were the smallest class of warship, but they were still large enough to carry a sizable crew and weapon compliment.

Edge cursed under his breath before continuing. "Thank you, Eddi. That's all useful information. What can you tell me about the message being broadcast?"

"It is encrypted. The only readable information is a tag denoting the intended recipient.

Petal. I have no point of reference for that data point and cannot provide you with any assistance in determining what or who Petal is."

River spoke up. "The message is for me. Eddi, can you decrypt any part of it?"

"Negative. I have never been provided with decryption software." The AI paused and then added, "I will have to discuss this oversight with Pilot Rem once I have been returned to her."

The pause this time was longer. "If that is still your intention. If it is not, I must inform you that I am equipped with anti-theft protocols."

River had to cover her mouth to stop herself from laughing at the AI's moment of drama.

"Relax your circuits, Eddi. We absolutely intend to give you back to Sevda." Edge looked like he wanted to reach through the connection and kick the AI in its nonexistent butt for going off topic.

"If Jens is sending this out, it's got to be a message for me. If that's the case, he thinks I have the key to decrypt it already."

"That makes sense, but let's hold off on that idea for now. There's something else we need to talk about, first."

She knew where this was going, but it surprised her that Edge was willing to talk about something that was clearly his fault. "How did he find us?"

"Exactly. He had to have tracked you somehow."

"What?" she uttered in shock. "That's not possible. I was in a cryo-pod inside a shielded cargo hold for the entire trip. There's no way he could have tracked me." She pointed at Edge. "He must have followed *you* here."

"That makes no sense at all. Jens sent you that first message either because he thought you'd come running back to him, or he expected you to bolt. Either way, he had a plan in place for finding you if you left Haven. I don't know how, but he's here, so that's got to be it."

Edge's assessment put her on the defensive. "You're

ignoring the fact that Nova Force is hunting you. They know what ship you're on, too. The Interstellar Armed Forces has always had information leaks. Every time they take out one spy, three more appear to take their place. The most likely scenario is that someone heard the chatter and reported it to their corporate handler. Jens or the people he's working with now got wind of it and decided to follow you. After all, the leader of the cyborgs on Haven wouldn't leave the colony without a good reason. Coming after a rogue cyborg would definitely count."

"And how did they track me here? I don't see how this is my fault," Edge argued.

"Eddi is, or was, corporate property. Do you really think they didn't have the means to track it down if they wanted to? And at the risk of repeating myself, this is why I told everyone not to *fraxxing* follow me."

Eddi interrupted before Edge could respond. "The vessel is positioning itself for orbital insertion. If I am to remain hidden, the position of this moon will put me in a communication blackout in forty-three minutes. Whatever you intend to do, it should be done quickly or I will not be able to assist."

"We need to listen to the message. That's the only source of information we have. Once we know what it says, we can make a plan."

"No," Edge snapped. "We are not listening to that message. *I* will, and you will not be in earshot when it happens."

"That's not your decision to make." She couldn't

believe he'd do this to her. He knew why she had to face Jens and how important this was to her.

"Yeah. It is. You said it yourself. You can't know that you haven't been compromised somehow. I won't let you risk yourself over a damned message. I'll listen to it and then come back and tell you everything I heard. I'm not the one he's obsessed with. Jens doesn't even know I'm here."

His words cut her deeply. Of all the beings she knew, he was the one she'd have sworn would never throw her own words back at her like that. *Compromised.* What's worse, was the fact that he could be right. That didn't make it hurt any less.

Her response came from her heart, unfiltered and raw. "Unless he followed you here," she protested. "And even if you're right, it's still my choice. This is my battle, and you can't tell me step back and let you handle it!"

"Damn it, River! I'm trying to protect you!"

She sat up and glared at him. Why couldn't he understand that his idea of protection was as much a prison as Reamus Station had been. If she wasn't free to make her own choices, she wasn't free at all. "For the last time, I don't need your protection. I never asked for it, and I don't want it! It's my life, Edge. You don't get to tell me how to live it."

They glowered at each other for several long seconds. Finally, Edge seemed to back down a little. "You're as stubborn as a *braxian* donkey. I'm going to take a walk. You do... whatever. Both of us agree not to do anything about the message until we're calmer. Deal?"

"Fine." She moved toward the opening that led to the

lower floor. "I'll grab a shower. I won't listen to the message until we talk again. Maybe by then I'll have figured out a way to make you see sense."

"You'd be the first to manage it," he joked. "We'll talk. I promise."

Trusting him was harder than she wanted it to be, but she nodded in reluctant agreement. "Don't take too long. We've still got to make a plan and relay it to Eddi before they are out of contact."

"I won't go far."

She went down the ladder first, slipping behind it to the sanitation cubby near the back of the shelter. Once inside, she shut the door and turned on the water. It was more of a drizzle than a proper flow, but the barely warm water washed away the sweat and dust of the day along with some of her anger.

As much as it pained her to admit it, Edge might have a point. How he'd made it, and what he'd said to her were another matter—one that threatened to derail any chance of a future between them. Ceding control to him in the bedroom was one thing, but if he expected her to obey him in all parts of their life, that wasn't much of a life at all.

Sadness and doubt distracted her for longer than she should have allowed. When she stepped out of the cubby, she expected Edge to be back.

He wasn't.

Maybe he was outside? Curious, she padded to the door and touched the panel to open it. The door mechanism whirred, but it didn't budge.

She tried again. This time, the whirr was

accompanied by a grinding noise and the panel flashed red.

"You asshole!" she yelled, her fist pounding on the door. "You promised me we'd talk first!"

14

Regrets gathered around Edge like a storm cloud as he ran across a string of sunbaked rocks that rose out of the desert. The rocks kept him safe from whatever predators moved beneath the sand, but not even his armor could shield him from the searing wind and unrelenting heat of this place.

It probably wouldn't help much against River when she realized that he'd jammed the door, locking her inside the shelter while he listened to the message alone. He hadn't done any permanent damage to the structure. The goal was to give him enough time to get clear and listen to whatever Jens had to say without putting River in harm's way.

It wasn't that he doubted her courage or her strength, but this wasn't a risk she should take. Not when he could do it instead. Edge had never been one of Jens' projects. He'd gone through his own hell at the hands of other researchers, but no one had messed with *his* mind.

It took him less than five minutes to reach a spot far

enough from camp that River wouldn't be able to catch up to him before he'd played the message. They still needed to work out a plan and fill Eddi in before they ran out of time, and he figured it would take more than a few minutes for River to finish yelling at him for what he'd done. He didn't feel good about what he'd done, but eventually she'd come to see that he'd made the right decision.

At least, that's what he hoped. A small voice in the back of his mind was telling him it wouldn't be that easy.

He took River's comm unit out of his pocket, switched it on, and set it to scan for any incoming signals. It locked on to one almost immediately. That had to be it.

A quick scan revealed the tag Eddi had mentioned. Petal. That was all the confirmation he needed. Edge tapped into his onboard systems and brought up every decryption program he'd been uploaded with or discovered on his own. Surely one of them would work.

The sun beat down on him without mercy as he waited for something to happen. When it did, it wasn't what he'd hoped for. Instead of the message from the mad scientist, he heard River's voice.

"You asshole! You promised to talk about this, and I believed you," she shouted through their internal comm channel. Her anger wasn't what struck him, though. It was the pain that underscored every word.

"I'm sorry," he sent back. *"And I didn't promise we'd talk about this. I promised we'd talk, and we will. I'll be back as soon as I can, and then we'll work this out."*

"No."

That single word filled him with a deep sense of dread. *"Minx? What do you mean? No what?"*

"I'm not sure," she admitted. *"But I'm also not sure we can work this out. You lied to me. You took away my choices and told me it was for my own good. Do you know who else used to say that to me?"*

He shook his head, as if she could somehow see him right now. *"It's not like that. I'm not like* him.*"*

"Prove it. Come back and we'll listen to the message together."

He nearly did it. The comm was halfway to his pocket and he was already moving before he caught himself and forced himself to stop.

"It's too big a risk. If you're compromised..."

Pain replaced the anger in her voice. *"Is this the future you see for us? You using what was done to me as justification for ignoring my wishes?"*

"It will only happen this one time. River, if it was any other battle, I'd let you fight it, but this is Jens we're talking about." He paused, swallowed hard, and then added, *"I need to keep you safe because you're precious to me. You are the one good thing in my life, minx. I can't lose you."*

Her answer was so slow in coming he wondered if she would say anything at all. When she did speak again, her tone was wry but wary. *"Did it every occur to you that I felt the same way?"*

He let go of a breath he'd held far too long and pushed some humor into his next reply *"Honestly? Not until right now. You can add it to my long list of personal flaws and epic screwups."*

She actually laughed a little. "*Believe me, I will.*" She paused for a beat and then asked, "*You're determined to do this without me. Aren't you?*"

"I am."

"*Then do it fast because I've got the door open and I'm headed your way. If I get there before you get that thing decrypted, we throw out your plan and go with mine. Deal?*"

Fraxx. She'd gotten out faster than he'd expected. "*I don't like it, but you have a deal. See you soon, love.*"

He broke the connection before he realized what he'd said. Love. The way he'd said it, it was more like a term of endearment. Only, he'd never used that word before. Not in any context he could remember.

The device in his hand beeped, pulling him away from that dangerous line of thinking.

He'd found the decryption key. The message was ready to play. Part of him considered waiting for River. She'd be here soon, and if he waited, it would go a long way toward mitigating the damage he'd done. It was probably the smart choice, but something in his gut kept insisting something about this message was dangerous.

He tapped the device once, and a voice he'd never wanted to hear again came through the speaker.

"Hello again, Petal. You were so clever, getting away from that vile planet so it would be easier for me to retrieve you. If you hadn't, I would have come for you eventually, but that prison planet you were forced to live on was a veritable fortress."

Edge listened to every smarmy, nauseating word and

thanked the stars River would never have to hear this crap.

"I know you're eager to see me again, but the ones I work for now don't know you like I do. They're not convinced that the improvements I made to you are working as intended." Jens uttered a phlegmy sigh. "They're wrong. Of course they're wrong. You are my masterpiece. My beautiful, perfect Petal. But they insist that I do this. Sleep well, my pet. We'll be together soon, and oh, I have such plans for us."

He crushed the comm unit as soon as the message ended. He didn't want to hear it again. Ever.

"Sleep well?" he mused as he dropped the pieces onto the sand. "What the hell does that..."

The bottom fell out of his mind before he finished speaking. As he fell into darkness, his last thought was of River.

She would never let him live this down.

15

———

Rɪᴠᴇʀ ʀᴀɴ ꜰᴀsᴛᴇʀ than she had in her life, determined to reach Edge before he had time to decode the message. Getting through the door had been relatively straightforward once she found the emergency override switch. In her agitated state she'd read the instructions wrong and spent an embarrassing amount of time looking in the wrong place. That was Edge's fault, too. Yelling at him had distracted her.

At least this time she'd taken the extra seconds needed to gear up properly. She was in full body armor with her pulse rifle slung over her shoulder and a blaster on her hip. The only thing she hadn't had time for was shoes. They were obviously *somewhere* in the camp, but she'd kicked them off right before he'd ordered her upstairs for another round of mind-melting sex, and they weren't on the floor after he locked her inside. Had Edge hidden them? Probably.

He must have taken both comm units, too, because

she hadn't found that either. Without either device, she had no way to contact Eddi.

"Stupid. Stubborn. Argh!" she ranted as she ran. The wind blasted the words away as soon as she said them, leaving her with a mouth full of dust in exchange.

She'd used their internal channel to ping him, so she knew which direction to go. That didn't tell her how far he'd gone in the time it had taken her to finish her shower and break herself free, though.

By now, her feet were probably in bad shape, but she couldn't feel them. She'd used one of her innate abilities to block the pain while still letting her feel enough to keep her footing as she ran.

She reached the top of yet another outcropping, slowing down slightly so she could scan the area for any sign of Edge. She spotted him easily enough, his dark armor standing out among the orange rocks.

She'd tried to reach him through their link several times already, but she did it again as she approached his location.

Still no response.

River stopped to assess the situation carefully. Edge lay face down, one arm trapped beneath him and the other splayed out to the side with the shattered remains of her comm unit lying nearby. Not a good sign.

She increased the magnification of her vision, looking desperately for some indication he was alive.

"Thank the stars. You're still breathing," she said, relief easing some of the tightness in her chest once she spotted the almost imperceptible movement.

If Edge heard her, he gave no sign. Nothing around

gave her any hint as to what had happened, but she already had a theory.

Kneeling beside him, she checked for a pulse and found one, slow but steady. He had no obvious injuries other than a bruise on his cheek where he'd hit the rocks when he fell. Her check also failed to turn up the second comm unit. He must have left it back at the camp. "He probably hid the *fraxxing* thing inside my boots. Wherever they are."

There was a lot she didn't know for certain, but the situation reminded her of what the Grays had done to Skye. They'd used a spoken command to knock her unconscious. It wasn't one of the ones they'd known about, and it had led to the discovery that Skye, River, and Talia, were all implanted with the *fraxxing* codes and behavior mods that made them sleeper agents.

But every cyborg in Haven had been scanned and any unidentified codes were scrubbed from their operating systems. That's why she'd been so paranoid and had used every opportunity to check herself. She was clean. So was Edge. She'd been there both times he'd been scanned. So what the *fraxx* had done this to him and how did she snap him out of it?

She moved beside his head, leaning over him so her lips were by his ear. "Wake up!" she yelled, feeling equal parts afraid and foolish.

When he didn't stir, she tried everything she could think of. She talked to him. Shouted at him. Shook him. When none of that worked, she tried various pain stimuli to try and wake him.

Tears of frustration and worry soaked her cheeks as

she did everything she could think of to rouse him, but in the end, she had to give up. She was out of time.

She got to her feet and then crouched down again and hauled Edge's unconscious body over her shoulders. "You owe me for this," she grunted as she strained to stand again. "And I will take my payment by telling you that I told you so every day for a month!"

The trip back to camp took longer than her mad dash to find Edge, but she still managed a decent speed. Keeping Edge balanced over her shoulders while jogging over the uneven rocks demanded her full attention and taxed her cybernetically enhanced body to limits she hadn't reached since she'd last been in combat.

When she finally made it back to camp, she was sweating and too tired to continue the tirade of curses she'd kept up the first half of the trek. Streaks of blood marked her footprints as she carried Edge into the storage tent. It wasn't as cool or as comfortable as the shelter, but the tent was large enough for her to set the big cyborg down and still be able to move around him.

It only took a few seconds to check his vitals again. No change. Which she took as an indication she was right about what had happened. As far as she could tell, Edge wasn't in immediate danger.

That done, River scoured the campsite, looking for the other comm device. And her *fraxxing* boots. She found them all in the same place. Edge had tucked them between the two cisterns of water sitting in the back of the storage tent, less than a meter from where she'd set him down.

She sat beside Edge, taking the weight off her injured

feet and grabbing a few minutes of rest. The way things were going, she might not get another chance to catch her breath.

Hoping Eddi hadn't miscalculated the amount of time it would be in range, she activated the unit and spoke. "Eddi. This is River. Are you receiving?"

"I am. Expected time until we lose contact is one hundred seconds. What do you require?"

Despite the need to hurry, she couldn't help but bark out a short, bitter laugh. "I need a lot more than you can provide, but I'm glad to hear from you, anyway. What's the situation up there?"

"The *Maggie-May-Dance* has entered orbit. A shuttle departed from that vessel and is on its way to the planet's surface. Based on its current speed and trajectory, it should land within a two-kilometer radius of your position in approximately twenty-seven minutes."

Veth. Jens had to be on that shuttle. Whatever had happened to Edge, the asshole doctor knew about it and was coming to collect his prize. *Her.*

She groaned as that realization led to another one. If Jens thought he'd captured her, he couldn't know that Edge was here. *Fraxx*-to-the-max! The bastard *had* tracked her somehow. She wasn't sure if she was more pissed off over the fact he'd managed to find her despite all her precautions or that Edge had been right all along.

"Eddi, how long until we're back in contact if you stay where you are?"

"Three hours and eighteen minutes."

Which meant either ordering Eddi come get them now despite the risk of the corvette in disguise blasting their only ride into oblivion or staying put and fighting. There was only one choice.

"Do everything you can to avoid detection and contact us again as soon as it's possible."

"I will do so. Stay safe. Pilot Rem would not be pleased of something happened to either of you." The AI paused. "Or to me."

"I'll do my best to make sure all of us get home safely. I promise," River said.

"Thank you for that reassurance. Communication blackout now commencing. Good luck."

Something about Eddi was definitely odd. She'd never heard of an AI wishing anyone good luck before, and the program seemed to have a keen interest in its own survival. That hinted at a level of self-awareness no artificial intelligence was supposed to have.

If she survived this current cluster-*fraxx*, she'd have to ask Sevda about it.

Turning her attention back to the needs of the moment, she shifted positions so that she was between Edge and one of the cisterns. It was time to try and wake him up again. If she failed this time? Well, she'd have to find a safe place to stash him while she dealt with Jens and whoever else was in that shuttle.

River got to her knees and cradled Edge's head in her hands. "I love you, you big stubborn idiot. Come back to me."

Nothing. But she hadn't really expected that would work.

"Okay then. Since romantic declarations of love aren't getting through, let's try something else."

She reached back with one hand and groped for the tap she knew was embedded halfway up the container. Once she found it, she cranked it open and let a torrent of water wash over them both. The contents of the cistern weren't chilled, but compared to the heat outside it was like being doused in ice water.

"Wake up!" she shouted at him, repeating the message at the same volume over their internal link.

She called to him several more times before accessing the file she'd hoped she'd never need. The one containing every piece of code she could find that pertained to putting the cyborgs into a dormant state along with the codes required to bring them back online. Countless hours of work had gone into this collection. It had started as a way of taking back control and had grown into a determined need to find some way to fight back if they ever came for one of her friends again.

She used their link to transfer it all to Edge. She didn't even know if it could be done this way, but it was all she had left to try.

"Please work," she whispered, not even sure who she was talking to. Maybe to the bits of code themselves, as if she could compel them by willpower alone.

A week ago, she'd wanted nothing more than to confront Jens on her own. To face her fears and the man who had inflicted them on her and make him pay. Now, things were different.

She still wanted revenge, but she didn't want to do this alone. She wanted Edge at her side. Was he perfect? The idea made her laugh. Hardly. But neither was she. After her surviving batch-siblings had turned their backs on her without even trying to get her back, she'd stopped trusting everyone. Until now.

Minutes ticked past as she waited for Edge to wake up. Hope kept her at his side long past the time she should have given up and gone on without him.

Finally, she leaned over him again. First, she brushed a tender kiss to his lips. Then, she filled her lungs and shouted at him one last time. "Edge! Wake up. I need you."

It was a foolish impulse that should never have worked.

But it did.

16

———

Someone was shouting. Maybe at him. What the hell did they want, and why were they so loud?

"Edge! Damn it, open your eyes."

They were definitely yelling at him. Rude. Who was that?

He opened his eyes to see River staring down at him, her eyes red like she'd been crying and her cheeks wet. Wait. Not just her cheeks. All of her.

"What?" he demanded and then realized he'd skipped a few words. "What the hell happened? Where are we? Why are you wet?"

He moved and water squelched out from under him. "Why am *I* wet?"

"Drastic times called for drastic measures. I dumped water on you to try and wake you up. As for your other questions, we're in the storage tent back at camp. I'm wet because I was down on the ground with you when I came up with the water idea. As for what happened?" She beamed at him before hugging him tightly. "This is the part where I get to say *I told you so.*"

"You did?" His recollection of events was still fuzzy. They'd argued. He'd left to go do... oh. Right. He'd listened to Jens' broadcast and then taken an unscheduled nap. They'd turned off his mind as easily as flipping a switch. He'd had no chance to fight back. Knowing someone else could do that whenever they wanted brought him back to his time at Reamus Station. The helplessness. The frustration. Only this was worse. On the station he could fight back or take a beating intended for someone else. This time? He'd gone down without even seeing the face of his enemy.

"The message was trapped somehow?" he asked and then pushed himself into a sitting position. Water pooled on the floor of the tent. Some of it had seeped into the open neck of his armor. Even his hair and beard were soaked.

"Looks like I'm not the only one who's been compromised." Her tone held no judgment, but he still winced as the words he'd thrown at her came back to bite him.

"How!" He wished he could punch someone right now. Anger was easier to deal with than this terrible sense of vulnerability.

"I don't know. We've both been scanned multiple times. There shouldn't have been a way for him to do that. But I didn't think he could have tracked me here, and clearly, he did." River stood up and then reached out a hand to him.

"I owe you an apology for that. You were right. He had to have followed me here somehow."

"I think my list of things I have to say sorry for is longer than yours." He folded River into his arms and kissed her. "So, yeah. I'm sorry."

"That's it?" She arched a brow once he let her speak again. "You are going to have to do better than that, but not right now. We've got about twelve minutes before our company arrives. So all personal discussions are on hold for now."

"Right." He nodded and kissed her again. Then he pulled back and looked around him as more details started to register. "Wait. You brought me back to camp? How?"

"I carried you. In bare feet because *someone* hid my boots. I tried everything I could think of to snap you out of whatever they did to you. Water. Yelling. I'm pretty sure I told you I loved you at some point, and not even that got a reaction. I don't know what finally worked, but I'm glad it did." She grinned at him. "I thought I was going to have do this without you."

"You told me you loved me?"

"I did. You slept through it."

"Next time, wait until I'm awake. I don't want to miss something that important." He stroked her hair back from her face. This gorgeous, brave, incredible female had saved him. After all his talk about being her protector and the way he'd tried to take away her choices because he thought he knew what was best for her... she'd saved him.

"I love you, River. Thank you for what you did today." He kissed her softly and then raised a hand to tap the side of his head. "That bastard turned me *off*. I thought I understood what it felt like to know someone else could control you like that. I was wrong. It's worse."

She kissed him back, her lips warm and soft against his. "I know a great counselor back home. Several, in fact. If you need to talk about it, I can put you in touch with them."

He growled at her, catching her lower lip between his teeth and nipping it gently before letting it go. "I don't need them. I have you. You know me better than anyone else. If I need to work through this new wrinkle, I promise I'll say something. Talking isn't really my go-to solution, though."

"Really? I hadn't noticed." Her tone was teasing, but there was a serious gleam in her eyes as she looked up at him. "No more charging off and doing it your way no matter what. And, yes, I am aware that applies to both of us."

"Next time, we'll try something different," he agreed.

"Like talking it through and actually listening to each other?"

He groaned. "If we do that, we won't argue. If we don't argue, we can't have make-up sex."

The look she gave him was hot enough to melt the sand outside into glass. "It's us, Edge. We're always going to argue. Then we'll get naked and work out our differences until the next time."

"That might be the sexiest thing I've ever heard."

"You're insane."

"Very possible. But you love me anyway. Don't you?"

he already knew the answer, but he wanted to hear her say it again.

"I do. But right now we have a pressing problem. We need a plan that keeps us alive while making Jens and his new friends dead."

"That's not a problem, minx. That's an opportunity. Like I said, talking isn't my go-to solution." He winked at her. "Kicking ass is more my style."

They geared up quickly, tossing out ideas that quickly coalesced into a workable plan. Edge couldn't stop himself from grinning the entire time. After all, any day he got to gear up and prepare for a fight was a good day, but this was so much more than just a fight. It was a chance to get some payback and avenge the ones he hadn't been able to protect. He'd always hoped he'd get this chance, but he'd never imagined he'd be here with River standing beside him.

Today wasn't just a good day. It was the best day of his life.

17

River held position above the camp site, watching. The sun was low enough on the horizon to cast long shadows that provided plenty of places for her to hide. Sealed inside her helmet, her heat signature was masked from sensors. The only thing they couldn't be sure of was how precisely Jens could track her position. If he realized she wasn't the one lying in the middle of camp right now, they'd have to go to Plan B. Unfortunately, they hadn't had enough time to come up with one.

"Did I mention how much I dislike this part of the plan?" Edge complained through their link.

To sell the illusion that she was the one sprawled out on the ground near the entrance to the camp, they had partially buried Edge in the sand. It hid his large size as well as the blaster they'd carefully concealed below his outstretched hand.

"It was your idea," she reminded him. They were restricted to internal comms to avoid being overheard by their unwanted guests. *"We could have just placed my*

armor on the ground so it looked like I was in it, but you didn't like that idea."

"Armor isn't useful if you're not wearing it."

"And that argument is why you're out there, slowly broiling to death. I understand it's an excellent way to cook meat, actually. It comes out quite tender."

"Great. Now I'm hot and hungry. Thanks so much, minx."

Bantering before battle wasn't something she'd done in a long time, but the easy back and forth was soothing in a way, and it helped to pass the time as they waited to spring their trap.

The shuttle had flown over the camp before setting down several hundred meters away, which meant they must have seen the body lying face down in the sand. All she and Edge could do now was wait and see what approach they took. If things went well, Jens and his cronies would stroll through the entrance and run smack into the various booby-traps she'd set up after her arrival. If they were more cautious and came over the rocks, this would be trickier.

River checked the data pad lying face-up near her feet. It showed the view from every security camera. Edge had managed to link his helmet's heads-up display to the same feed, meaning he saw what she saw despite him being face down in the sand.

"And here they come," Edge sent at the same second she saw the new arrivals come into view.

She watched and tried to take in as many details as she could. There were six of them. Five had weapons up and walked with the smooth, heel-toe motion of trained soldiers. All of them were the same height and general build. They looked human, she decided—all male and possibly clones.

The sixth member of the group wore a steel gray ship-suit instead of armor and struggled to keep up with the others. She recognized the way he moved before she even saw his face. Dr. Troyan Jens.

Her grip on the pulse rifle tightened, though she kept her finger well away from the trigger.

"*Easy, minx,*" Edge sent, his tone soft and soothing.

River made a conscious effort to exhale and loosen her fingers. "*I'm good. It's a shame he's in the back. I would have liked to see him get fried by that first trap.*"

"*You and me both. Speaking of which, they're getting close enough someone is going to get lit up in the next minute or so.*"

River moved to the edge of the shadow she was using for cover and stood on her toes so she could see what happened next with her own eyes instead of through the camera. Though the distance was greater, her visual acuity allowed her to see more detail than the camera.

Each of the soldiers had a rectangular square of gray fabric on their chest that probably showed their name or identification number, but that was it. None of them had any rank insignia or patches to indicate unit, branch, or even corporate affiliation.

"*These guys are ghosts. No identifying markers at all.*"

Edge didn't get a chance to answer before the soldier in the middle of the group stepped onto the electrified plate buried beneath the sand. His body spasmed as the current tore through him, his back arching with bone-breaking violence.

His teammates reacted instantly, raising weapons and taking up defensive stances as if expecting an attack. None of them even looked at their comrade when he collapsed into a lifeless heap.

"*One down,*" Edge sent.

The remaining soldiers held their ground for another minute before lowering their weapons. They left the body where it lay, making sure to give it and the surrounding area a wide berth.

Jens hadn't moved. He simply stared like he couldn't understand what had happened.

Eventually, one of the soldiers turned back to retrieve him, guiding him around the corpse with brusque, impatient gestures.

Jens followed as best he could, but she could see he was rattled by what had happened. Had he really deluded himself into thinking she was eager to see him? Edge had told her what was in the broadcast, but it was still hard to believe the scientist thought she actually came out here to make it easier for him to find her.

"*Do you think Jens knows those traps are meant for him?*" she sent to Edge.

"*I'm sure he's doing his best to convince himself you were trying to protect yourself from the local wildlife. That male's brain is broken.*"

The group moved on, but their progress was much slower. One of them was pushed to the front by the others, who hung several meters back as their chosen sacrifice prodded the sand with the butt of his rifle before taking each step.

If she'd used the same trap again, the tactic might have worked, but River knew better than to repeat the same trick twice in a row.

The bounding mine she'd buried in the passage was set deep enough to avoid the soldier's simplistic detection methods. Multiple pressure sensors spanned the gap with only a narrow path left clear. As the first soldier stepped into the trap, she caught herself wincing in anticipation of what came next.

Three. Two. One... the mine activated, propelling the explosive payload out of the sand. It rose about a meter before detonating, hurling metal shrapnel in every direction.

All four soldiers dropped to the ground, flailing and screaming as they clutched at their shredded armor and torn flesh.

Edge was on his feet and running a split-second after the detonation. His job was to finish off any survivors. They weren't taking prisoners today, and they couldn't leave witnesses.

River was on the move too, launching herself off the ledge and into the air. She hit the ground with enough force to drive her to one knee, but it didn't slow her down. Nothing would, not when she was so close to ridding herself of Jens forever.

She covered the distance in seconds, ignoring the four males on the ground as Edge moved between them, his blaster firing every few seconds as he put them out of their misery.

She found Jens curled into a fetal position not far behind the others. He'd fared better than they had but not by much. Distance and the armor the others wore had reduced the amount of shrapnel that struck him, but his ship-suit had offered no protection.

Blood soaked the sand as he pawed weakly at his stomach. She leaned in and confirmed her first impression. Yeah, that was definitely his stomach, along with several loops of intestines and what was probably part of his liver. She waited to feel something. Satisfaction, maybe, or a sense of relief, but all she felt was tired.

It wasn't what she'd expected, but it was enough.

Jens raised his head to stare at her with eyes glazed over with pain and shock. "Petal? Is that you?"

She didn't answer. She had nothing left to say to this waste of oxygen.

"My pet, I knew you'd come. You must help me." He reached for her with a gore-soaked hand.

Apparently she had something to say after all. "No."

"But, Petal. I came all this way for you. You're my shining gem. My..." He coughed, the action pushing another loop of intestine into view.

"I'm not your anything. I never was." She glanced skyward, noting the position of the sun. It would set soon, marking the end of her time on this planet.

That thought triggered another, an idea forming as the sky began to glow in a glorious vista of colors.

She walked around Jens' feet, picking up the one that looked the least injured. "What are you doing?" he asked.

She tightened her grip on his ankle and started walking, dragging him behind her.

"Petal!" he screamed, her name twisting into something incoherent as pain stole what was left of his mind.

It only took a few minutes to reach the point where the rocks that protected her camp gave way to open sand. She dragged him a few meters farther from the safety of the rocks before dropping his foot.

"Petal..." he croaked, his eyes already dimming as death closed in.

"My name is not Petal." She told him, her voice so cold and flat she hardly recognized it. She leaned close, ignoring the stench of death that clung to him. She wanted him to see her face as she spoke the last words he'd ever hear. "My name is River!"

She straightened, turned, and hurried back toward the rocks, leaving him sprawled across the sand. The sky was truly beautiful now, a dazzling display of colors no mortal artist could ever hope to duplicate.

The first scream came about less than a minute later, followed by another and another. If there were words in the sounds, she couldn't make them out.

Edge met her part way back to camp. The moment he saw her, he broke into a run, barely slowing as he reached her and pulled her into his arms. "Are you alright?" he asked, running his hands over body as if checking her for injuries.

"He didn't hurt me," she said. "He won't hurt anyone ever again."

"Good." He stroked her hair gently as he brushed

tiny kisses over her face. "I put them all down, and when I looked up, you were gone. Where did you go?"

His gentle touch and deep concern surprised her, but not as much as the tears that flowed down her cheeks as she rose on her toes to kiss him.

"I ended it."

Another wail of terror and pain tore through the air, and Edge frowned in confusion.

"You left him alive?"

River shook her head, her fingers smoothing away the creases in his brow. "He won't be for long. I left him for the sand sharks."

Edge shot her a feral grin before kissing her hard.

"You are a dangerous female, River. I had no idea."

She laughed as something loosened in her chest, letting her breathe deeply for the first time in what felt like a lifetime. "Neither did he."

They stood like that for as long as they dared, aware that the danger wasn't over yet.

Edge eventually broke the silence. "Ready to go home, minx?"

As much as she wanted that, it wasn't the right time. "We can't go home, Edge. Not yet. But we can't stay here, either." She took his hand in hers. "I think it's time we got off this dust bowl. Are you ready to leave?"

"More than ready. C'mon, my dangerous beauty, we're off to steal a shuttle and get the hell off this rock."

Dangerous beauty? Oh yeah. She liked the sound of that.

18

Sneaking up on the shuttle turned out to be the easiest part of this mission. The pilot wasn't even on board when they arrived. He was twenty meters from the open hatchway, sitting on a small cluster of rocks and taking pictures of the sunset with an imager. Edge had dropped him with a single shot from his pulse rifle.

They'd cleared the vessel quickly, the two of them working together as if they'd always been a team. It was one more reason to kick himself in the ass for fighting his attraction to River for as long as he had. Everything was easier when they were together.

Once they had the ship, Edge went to work closing the hatch and ensuring it was properly sealed.

"Confession time," he said. "I never got even a basic flight instruction package. My corporate overlords assumed I'd just order someone else to fly me and my team wherever they needed us to go. That's why I needed a ship with a high-level AI." He winked at River. "So this is me, ordering you to fly us the hell out of here."

She grinned. "Yes, Commander."

Damn, he loved it when she said that.

It was also good to see her smile. His worry for her hadn't ended when she'd come back from taking care of Jens. He hadn't liked the distant look in her eye, almost as if she'd left part of herself out in the sand.

That look wasn't there now. This was the River he'd finally gotten to know, and he loved everything about her.

"I'll get us in the air, but the second we take off, that corvette is going to expect an update. Unless you can do a decent impression of Dr. Jens, that is not a good idea."

Edge raised his voice to an unmanly squeak and quavered. "Do you think they'll believe this is him?"

"Not a chance." River snorted with laughter. "So we're going with the tried and true 'fly like we stole it' approach and hope Eddi can pick us up?"

"We *did* steal it," Edge pointed out. "And I'll contact Eddi right now."

"You should strap in first. Remember, this is my first time flying solo."

He couldn't tell if she was kidding, but he dropped into the nearest seat and buckled himself in. Just in case.

Despite her warning, the shuttle lifted off smoothly. Once he was certain she had things handled, he contacted Eddi and then asked River to route the link through the shuttle's comms so she could be involved in the conversation.

Arranging for the scout ship to meet them as quickly as possible was straightforward. Figuring out a way to get aboard was a bigger challenge given they didn't have vac-suits, but Eddi had a solution.

"I am equipped with an emergency umbilical tube intended for this type of situation. Once activated, it will unfold and seal against the hull of your shuttle. The adhesive process for this is not designed for long-term use, but it should hold long enough for both of you to cross over."

"You're certain it will hold? Why can't we dock this ship alongside you and match the airlock doors?"

"I'm a scout ship. I am not designed for that kind of connection."

Edge bit back a laugh. The AI sounded slightly horrified at the idea of hooking onto another ship.

"Okay. Okay. It was an honest question. No need to get your circuits in a bunch."

"You are not making sense, Passenger Edge. Should I prepare the med system to check you for head injuries once you are on board?"

"No med systems," he snapped. "I'm fine, but even if I wasn't, my medi-bots would deal with it." The last thing he wanted was to have the AI taking scans and offering medical advice.

River piped up from the cockpit. "Actually, I might need the med-system. I tore up my feet badly and I suspect there's a lot of sand and other debris in the cuts. My medi-bots can clean it all up eventually, but I'll heal faster if it's done soon."

"Of course, Pilot River. I will prepare for your treatment once you arrive."

"Wait a second. Why am I just Passenger Edge, but River gets to be called Pilot?"

The damned AI sounded absolutely smug as it

replied, "Because my records indicate River has preliminary flight qualifications. You do not."

River's laughter filled the air. "We'll rendezvous with you in fourteen minutes, Eddi. The other ship has stopped trying to hail us and is on an intercept course, but they won't get here in time. Please begin calculating jump coordinates for a random destination at least five light-years away. That will give us time to work out where we're really going."

"Calculations beginning now. Will there be anything else?"

"No. Please get to the meeting point as fast as you can. The sooner we're safe, the sooner we can get you back to Sevda."

The AI made a pleased humming sound. "That would be my preferred outcome."

"Ours too," Edge chimed in.

With the preliminary issues out of the way for the moment, he moved on to his next concern. "How bad are you hurt, minx?"

"I'll live. But if I don't deactivate the nerve-block soon, the system will do it for me. I'd rather finish my treatment before the pain comes back."

He was out of the harness and on his feet in seconds. "Why didn't you say anything?" he demanded as he barged into the cockpit.

"I did. I told you I carried you back to camp barefoot because you hid my *fraxxing* boots."

He growled and ran a hand through his hair, leaving it in spikes that reflected his current mood. "We need to work on our communication."

She flicked an amused glance over her shoulder at him. "What happened to the man who complained if we stopped arguing we'd stop having make-up sex?"

"He's gained some perspective since then." He placed a hand on her shoulder, the simple touch grounding him.

"We did have a busy day," she agreed. Without another word, she turned her head to kiss his fingers.

"Yeah, we did. And it's not over yet."

"Not even close." River nodded to the copilot's seat. "Since you're here, we should talk about what comes next."

"We don't have a lot of options." He sat down without bothering to strap in this time. "As much as I hate to say it, we can't do this alone. We're going to need help."

"I agree. As it happens, Hezza left me a good-bye present—a comm relay buoy in orbit around the planet. She set it up so I had way to reach her if needed. I think that time has come."

"Agreed. It might take a while for her to get the message, though. I'm not sure where she is, but it will be a long way from here...or anywhere that Nova Force might find her."

"I know. But it's a start. Now we need to figure out what to tell her. Starting with where we're headed."

"Where do you think we should go?"

He expected her to suggest Vardarian space or maybe another isolated planet. Instead, River shot him a mischievous smile.

"I think we need to talk to the one person who might be able to see a way for us to get out of this mess."

He tried to figure out who she meant but drew a total blank. "Who?"

"I'll give you a hint. She's the only other cyborg to ever leave Haven."

Fraxx. Why didn't he think of that? "Chance!"

"Exactly. Which means we need to get to The Drift. Eddi, can you chart a course that will get us to Defiance Station? You can make the jump as soon as we're on board. Oh, and send an encrypted message to our friends back on Haven to let them know our destination. But only if you're sure these assholes can't intercept it."

"Of course, Pilot River. I will begin immediately."

Edge broke in as another idea took root. "Don't take us directly there, Eddi. Plot a roundabout route that lets us drop out of jump space several times. It will take longer, but it will keep the assholes on our tail from working out where we're going quickly. The more time we keep them guessing, the less time they'll have to send someone to intercept us."

River nodded. "Good plan. Eddi, can you map a route that also takes us close to a couple of repeater stations? That way we can check for messages and send some of our own.

It wasn't the best plan he'd ever come up with, but it would have to be good enough.

Edge looked at River and grinned to himself. It was going to be another long trip to get to their destination, but this time, he had a long list of ways he intended to pass the time.

All of them involved River, nudity, and orgasms.

19

———

RIVER LEFT the shuttle with reluctance. Not because she wanted to stay and get caught but because it meant the end of her first solo flight. Once they were aboard the scout ship, Eddi would handle the flying. She'd planned to spend some time in the cockpit, though, learning anything Eddi wanted to teach her about the ins and outs of piloting.

The AI activated the jump-drive within seconds of their arrival. It jettisoned the tunnel they used to cross over the moment the airlock door sealed.

"We are underway. The other ship has changed its transponder and is now appearing as an unnamed Viper class vessel registered to El-Corp, which appears to be a holding company."

"Three guesses who the real owner is," Edge said. He was already busy taking off his body armor and dumping it in a pile in an open corner.

"My gut says it's Torex," River said. She was ready to

ditch her armor as well and happily shed the protective but restricting gear.

"That would be my first guess, too, but it could belong to anyone affiliated with the Shadows."

They looked at each other, both dusty, sweaty, and stained with blood.

"Please tell me this sweet little ship has a shower?" she asked.

"It does." Edge reached out a hand. "Come with me, minx."

She took his hand and let him lead her through the confines of the ship. It wasn't large, but the design was well thought-out with a balance of practicality and comfort. The sanitation cubby was no exception. After so long living and sleeping in her cramped shelter, the ship felt almost palatial by comparison.

There was even a separate shower stall, and Eddi confirmed it could recycle the water fast enough to allow them unlimited use.

Edge stopped her just inside the door. "Strip off and give me all your clothes. I'll put everything in the recycler and have Eddi use it to make you something new."

His offer surprised her, but she wasn't going to argue. She never wanted to see any piece of her current outfit again.

He took her things and disappeared, which gave her time to use the facilities and rinse the dust out of her mouth. When he returned, he was as naked as she was, his cock rising from between his legs and a gleam in his eyes that told her she wouldn't be showering alone.

"Eddi, engage privacy mode," he instructed.

"Engaged," the AI stated before lapsing into silence.

"Now, let's get you off your poor feet," he said. Before she could protest, he caught her by the hips and lifted her onto a small stretch of counter beside the sink.

"Stay," he told her, grinning as he leaned in to kiss her lightly on the mouth.

She nodded, faintly amused and somewhat embarrassed by this unexpected treatment. He turned on the shower, fiddling with the knobs until he was satisfied with the temperature. Then he pulled a towel from underneath the sink and soaked it in the warm water.

"I could rinse them off in the shower. That should get most of the sand and grit out."

"We'll get to that," he said as he kneeled in front of her. "Let me take care of you."

"Okay," she said, aware of the warmth creeping up her cheeks.

He took one foot in his hands and wiped the dirt away with more care than she thought him capable of. Slowly and gently he cleaned each cut and abrasion, muttering darkly as he took in the damage she'd done. Bright spots stained the towel, but not as much as she'd expected.

"The medi-bots did a better job than I expected. I thought the dirt would slow the healing process."

"It has, but I can clean this up enough the medi-bots can manage the rest." He looked up at her, his ice-blue eyes filled with concern. "How's the pain?"

"I haven't dropped the nerve-block yet," she admitted. "I got a little distracted by my very sexy nurse."

"Your sexy nurse says it's time. If it hurts too much,

I'll get you something to help, but you know we can't keep those blocks in place for too long."

"I know." She braced herself for the discomfort and deactivated the block.

"How is it?"

"Not bad at all." River wiggled her toes. "At this rate I'll be healed up by morning. Does this mean I can take that shower now?"

"Not yet. Let me finish up."

He went back to work, and again she was surprised by his gentleness. Even without the nerve-block, she never felt more than a brief bite of discomfort.

When he finished, he pulled open a small slot and dropped the towel inside. "Laundry chute," he explained.

"Nice. Sevda put some serious money into upgrading this ship."

"She did." He held his arms out to her. "Come here, minx. I'll carry you to the shower."

It was less than a meter away, but she knew better than to argue with him right now. Once he had her, he turned and carried her over to the steady flow of gloriously hot water.

"I'd forgotten how nice it feels to have a proper shower. The one back at camp couldn't manage more than a drizzle of warm water."

"This is much better," he agreed. "What about the shower at your place back home? Is it big enough for two?"

She laughed. "It is. Is that your way of asking if I'll share my shower with you?"

"Maybe. I always liked the idea of having a place with a view of the river."

"You could have picked one with a view. Why didn't you?"

As they talked, the water poured over both of them, sluicing away the sand and sweat. The cuts on her feet stung a bit, but the water would finish cleaning the wounds and let them heal properly.

"Because I didn't care which house I lived in. I didn't think any of them would ever feel like a proper home. It would just be a safe place for me to rest. Why would I take one of the ones with a pretty view away from someone who would actually appreciate it?"

She cupped his cheek in her hand. "Because you deserve nice things, too. You don't have to sacrifice everything for us, you know. We want you to be happy, too. All of us. Not just the cyborgs but everyone who knows you."

His eyes filled with a mix of confusion and longing. "Yeah?"

"Yes, you big idiot."

"You know what would make me very happy right now?" he asked, his lips almost touching hers.

"I think I can guess." She closed the distance and kissed him before he could. "Whatever you want, Commander. It's all yours."

"All I need is you. Not your surrender, though you know I love that. But this time, I want you. No demands. No submission."

She shivered despite the hot water flowing over her. "I'd like that too."

He set her down then, watching her carefully in case her feet were still to tender. "I'm fine," she assured him.

"In that case..." He wrapped a strong arm around her waist and pulled her in for a searing kiss. She moaned into his mouth and reached between them to wrap her fingers around the hard shaft of his cock.

He bucked against her hand, his body shuddering as he groaned her name. His cock twitched and pulsed as she stroked him, the twining of their tongues a promise of what was to come.

"What do you need?" he asked, his voice all gravel and steel.

"You. I want you inside me."

Edge raised his head to smile at her, his eyes bright with desire. "As my minx wishes."

He kissed her again. This time it was a slow, heated kiss that made her heart pound and her toes curl against the tile floor. This kiss went on forever, leaving her drunk with passion as he tasted and teased her.

She worked his cock with her hand, matching the slow, easy heat of his movements with her own.

Eventually his mouth left hers to trace the line of her jaw, down to her throat, and then lower still. The soft touch of his lips blended with the flow of water over her skin until it all blurred into one glorious whole.

Her body sang with need, but still he continued his way slowly down until his mouth was on her breasts.

She released his cock to bury her fingers in his hair, holding him close as she kissed him with a hunger she'd never felt before.

Edge laughed and reached up to catch her by the

wrist. He raised her arms over her head and held them there as he used his free hand to tweak one sensitive nipple. "In a rush. Are we?"

"Yes," she huffed at him.

"Soon. But first..." He leaned down and drew her nipple into the heat of his mouth. She arched into him, craving more of his touch. More of *him*.

He gave her what she needed, but soon his hand drifted lower, sliding down her stomach to her pussy. With a low growl, he pushed one finger into her slick folds.

"Yes. Like that. Please," she whispered as he stroked her. Without thinking, she moved her feet further apart, opening herself to his questing fingers.

He circled her clit with a callused fingertip, his tongue mirroring the motion as he laved her breast.

"I love you," she whispered. Then she pulled her hands free of his hold and buried them in the thick mane of his hair.

Edge released her breast and raised his head to stare into her eyes. "Say that again."

"I love you."

He flicked her clit with his fingers again and then pulled his hand away. "I am the luckiest man in the galaxy. And for the record, I think I've loved you since the first day we met."

When he kissed her this time, her world went up in flames.

"This shower is too *fraxxing* small," he announced a few moments later.

She didn't protest when he picked her up again. She

simply held on as he stalked out of the shower. "Where are we going?"

"Bed," he declared, "and I don't plan on letting you leave it again until tomorrow."

She kissed him again. "You won't hear any complaints from me."

The bed was bigger than the shower but not by much. It was a double wide bunk that took up one wall and most of the floor space.

He set her down in the middle of the mattress, kissed her once, and then covered her with his body. She parted her thighs in welcome as he settled over her, his hard cock coming to rest just outside where she needed him most.

"Tell me what you need," he coaxed her, his cock throbbing as it pressed against her entrance.

"I already told you," she protested. "But I'll say it again. I want you."

"I will never get tired of hearing that." Edge kissed her again, and then he was inside her.

His groans filled the room as their bodies merged, her flesh giving way to his thick length. As his hips touched hers, she arched her back, taking him deeper still, and was rewarded with a wave of pleasure so intense she gasped.

"Perfect," he whispered, the word a caress as heated as any kiss. Then he was moving, each thrust slow as he buried himself inside her, only to withdraw until she ached with the loss of contact.

They danced together for ages, the pleasure building as they moved in harmony, each giving and taking in equal measure.

When it was all too much, she told him so. Not in words, but with small cries and needy moans that spurred him to move faster, to take her to the edge and let her soar.

Faster. Harder. Deeper. He drove himself into her like a force of nature. The pace grew wilder, and she felt his cock thicken as he neared the breaking point.

Edge threw back his head and shouted, his face a mask of ecstasy as he lost himself in her body. She followed him into the maelstrom, her cries blending with his.

When her senses returned, she opened her eyes to find him looking down at her with an expression of pure primal satisfaction.

"I was wrong. I'm not keeping you in bed until tomorrow," he said, his eyes twinkling.

"No?" she teased. "So I can get up right now?"

"Absolutely not. You're staying right here for two days. Maybe three."

She laughed and settled deeper into the mattress as a sense of deep contentment and joy filled her heart. "Yes, Commander."

20

———

FOR THE FIRST time he could remember, space travel didn't bore him. Two weeks after their flight from River's camp, he was rested, relaxed, and happier than he'd ever imagined possible.

They'd dropped into normal space twice. Each time staying only long enough to send a brief, heavily encrypted message to a relay buoy positioned along one of the busier shipping lanes. While it had been a long shot, they checked each one for messages from someone they knew, but there was nothing. The message they left behind was always the same, and they could only hope the right people would see it and understand. Chance, was the message, a clue to their destination and a request for anyone who read it to let Chance know what they were doing.

They were coming up on their next transition to normal space soon, but they had a few minutes before it happened. He had something he wanted to give River, and this felt like the right time.

She was in the cockpit, which wasn't a surprise. She spent hours there, practicing flight sims and learning anything she could from Eddi about flying a starship.

"If you spend many more hours in here, you're going to be a qualified ship pilot before we get home," he told her.

"That's what Eddi says, too." She rose from her seat to greet him with a kiss. "So I guess I have a new job when I get back." Her brow furrowed. "If we get back. I mean, I know we will eventually, but ..."

"But we've still got Torex chasing us, and so far no one else has reached out. It might take longer than we want to get this sorted."

"I know. I thought we'd have heard something by now. Maybe the messages haven't arrived yet?"

"Maybe." He stroked her cheek. "But I'm glad we've had this time together."

"Me too."

"I've realized something," he said, not sure how to put his feelings into words. Neither one of those things were his strong suite. He was better *doing* something than talking about it.

River waited for him to continue. "I don't want to do things alone anymore. I want to do them with you." He opened his hands and lifted them so she could see the gift he had for her. The necklace hung from his fingers, the simple pendant swinging gently.

"This is for you."

She took it from him, her expression soft with wonder. "It's a heart. But what's it made of?"

"Sand. When I took your clothes that first day, I

shook out all the sand from them, and from my clothes, too. I had the fabricator turn it into this." He touched the pendant, making it spin at the end of the chain.

"It's a reminder of all we went through and where we were when I finally accepted the truth—that I was in love with you."

Her smile was brighter than a hundred suns. "That is the sweetest thing you've ever said. Thank you. Will you... put it on?"

"Yes." He lifted the chain in both hands and lowered it over her head. "You're mine now, minx."

She touched the pendant with one hand, her eyes alight with love. "I always was. I just didn't know it yet."

Eddi's voice shattered the moment. "We will drop into normal space in ten seconds."

"*Fraxx*! Eddi, what happened to the two-minute warning?" River asked.

"I didn't want to interrupt. I do not understand much about biological beings' mating rituals, but Sevda has told me several times not to interrupt when one occurs."

Edge spluttered. "That wasn't a mating ritual."

"It certainly looked like one to me," Eddi retorted. "And we have now returned to normal space. I am scanning for the relay buoy."

A small pause was followed by an ear-shattering alarm and Eddi's voice calling out, "Proximity alert! A ship has decloaked in close proximity. Alert! Alert!"

"Eddi, mute that alarm and tell me what's happening!" River demanded.

The ship fell silent instantly.

"Eddi?" River asked. "What the hell is happening?"

"We are being hailed."

"By who?" Edge demanded.

Eddi spoke again. "System override initiated. Incoming message."

He stood behind River, determined to stare down whatever this new threat might be.

"Is this thing working?" a new voice demanded.

River relaxed and then burst out laughing. "It's alright, Edge. I think the cavalry has finally arrived. Eddi, put them on screen and open the channel so I can respond."

The main screen flickered to life. It showed a human female with silver hair and an annoyed expression. "I can't tell if this is sending or not."

River raised a hand in greeting. "Hello, Phylomenia. It's been a long time."

The older woman smiled, and it was as if ten years melted off her age. "River! Good to see you, girl. You've been busy. Haven't you?"

"You could say that. I hope you're here to help us out and not to arrest us," River replied.

Edge still wasn't sure what was going on, but River seemed to know the female, so he stayed quiet.

A human male appeared on the monitor. He looked familiar, but Edge couldn't recall his name. "We should arrest both of you, considering what you've been up to. I clearly recall a time you promised that none of the cyborgs from Reamus would be running around the galaxy unsupervised, yet here you are."

River tensed. "Colonel Archer, I can explain."

That was it. Archer. The man who had helped

orchestrate the deal that allowed the Vardarians to claim Liberty as long as they took in Edge and the others. If he tried to arrest them... His hand curled into a fist. Not happening.

Phylomenia waved her hand. "Don't listen to him. Scotty isn't a colonel anymore. He retired, so he couldn't arrest you even if he wanted to." She turned to glare at the former colonel. "And we don't want to do that."

Edge relaxed a little. Whatever was going on, Archer wasn't the one he needed to worry about.

Phylomenia turned to the screen again and smiled. "We're here because Chance sent us to find you. She said we were your best shot at getting clear of whatever mess you're in. So, where's the asshole hunting you?"

"Dead," River said without a hint of remorse.

"Good. So, if he's dealt with, why are you here instead of on you way back to Haven?" Phylomenia asked.

"Because he was working with the Shadows. The ship Jens was on is still chasing us. It's a Viper class warship registered to a corporation that has to be a shell company. When we first saw it, it showed as a commercial freighter named the *Maggie-May-Dance*. It only dropped the fake transponder once we made it off the planet and it gave chase."

"I told you they wouldn't give up easily!" a third voice called from somewhere off screen.

Phylomenia shook her head. "Yes. Yes. You're brilliant. You'll get a cookie later."

"That's not what I want, and you know it, Mena."

The woman smirked. "Fine. Orgasms later instead of cookies."

"Who was that?" River asked.

"Garrett Michaels." Phylomenia held up her left hand. "I got married. That's husband number two."

Archer buried his face in his hands. "This is why I wanted to have this conversation without the two of you on the bridge."

Edge burst out laughing. "I wasn't sure at first, but I think I'm going to like you all."

Eddi interrupted again, though this time it kept the alarms at a reasonable noise level.

On the other ship's bridge, red lights flashed, indicating they were getting the same warning.

"Warning. Jump point detected. Another ship is about to transit into normal space."

Scott Archer scowled. "Friends of yours?"

"The only friends we have out here is you," River said.

Archer nodded. "Then I think it's time we said hello. Get that little ship of yours tucked in behind the *Bat*. I'll extend the shields to protect you. We'll talk soon."

As the message ended, Phylomenia called out "Enjoy the show!"

Once he was sure the connection was severed, Edge moved deeper into the cockpit, already looking for the newly arrived ship. "Well, that was interesting."

River nodded, her eyes on the same screen as his. "Phylomenia is something else. She's the reason we knew about Liberty at all. She's friends with a lot of people, including the princess, Sevda, and Zura. You remember her?"

"Zura? Yeah, I do. She came to visit the colony after Astek Station was decommissioned. She's married to a pair of cyborgs. Good males. Solid fighters."

"That's her."

"You know a lot more humans than I do," he commented.

"We can change that."

While they talked, Eddi positioned them exactly where Archer had instructed.

"Do you think they're talking to the other ship?" Edge asked.

Pulse cannon fire slammed into the shield protecting them. "I think they're done talking," River said.

When Archer's ship fired, the blast didn't bounce off the shield. It tore right through it and took out a good portion of the other ship's lower deck.

"Do I want to know why a retired colonel is flying around the galaxy with that kind of firepower?" he asked.

"Probably not. Right now, I'm just glad he's on our side."

They watched in horror as airlocks all over the ship opened suddenly. Bodies were blown out into the void, along with the ship's atmosphere.

"*Re'veth.* They killed the crew?" River asked.

The channel between their ship and Archer's reactivated. "Are you seeing this?" Phylomenia asked, her face pale.

"We are. Did they say anything? Why did they fire?" River asked.

"We hailed them but never got a reply."

Archer chimed in. "Oh, they replied all right. But with weapons instead of words."

"But why kill everyone?" River asked.

Phylomenia answered this time. "Because dead men tell no tales."

"The dead don't share secrets, but sometimes databases do. We need to get Nova Force out here to retrieve the wreckage and see what they can get off the systems. Even if they wiped them, I'm sure Magi can get something we can use. They didn't have time to do a complete job."

River sighed and leaned into him. "So, it's over now?" she asked.

"For now," Phylomenia said.

"The IAF are going to have some questions you need to answer," Archer stated. "But you'll be alright. After all, you were the victim of a corporate conspiracy."

"I was?" River cocked her head in confusion, but Edge saw where this was going. It really was going to be alright.

"You were," Garrett called from off screen.

"Definitely," Archer stated firmly.

"Oh yes," Phylomenia agreed.

River nodded. "Ah, yes. I was."

Edge asked the next question. "So, where to now?"

Phylomenia smiled. "To the same place you were already heading. We're going back to The Drift."

Edge considered that for a moment and then bent down to kiss River's cheek. It didn't matter where they went, so long as they did it together.

"Sounds good," he said. "I've always wanted to see that place. I've heard a lot about it."

EPILOGUE

Defiance Station wasn't open for business yet, but it was already a busy place. River missed the old station, but she had to admit the new one was full of promise, not to mention state-of-the-art technology and a security system that was second to none. Since the last one had to be decommissioned after an attack by the Gray Men, no one was taking chances.

River sat near the viewscreens that covered the outer wall of the new Nova Club. Workers and bots were setting up the casino area while staff members familiarized themselves with the new layout and menu. There were hints of the old place scattered around. The walls were the same dark blue, and the new floor lit up in swirling patters of light when you stepped on it, just like the old place. And of course, the owners hadn't changed. Kit, Luke, and Cynder still ran the place with the help of their mates and friends.

River had already caught up with them, but at the

moment, she sat next to Edge, who watched the assembly of the various gambling tables with interest.

Chance had been delayed by some last-minute meeting, but she was on her way to meet them now. River didn't mind. It gave her some much-needed time to reflect on everything that had happened since they'd met up with Phylomenia and her husbands.

Archer had been right. Valuable intel had been stored on the ship's computers. They'd uncovered a few code names and references that may lead to arrests, but the biggest discovery was the existence of yet another research station.

The military had already dispatched ships to investigate, and despite being retired, Archer had somehow managed to get himself, his wife, and his husband included. They'd already left, though River had Phylomenia's word that she'd be in touch once she had information to share.

They now knew for certain that Torex, the mining corporation that had lost their claim to Liberty when the Vardarians took it over, owned the ship that Jens had been on. They claimed the ship had been stolen years ago, but investigations were ongoing. Nova Force had several teams looking for connections between the corporation and the Shadows.

For River, the most important information recovered from the ship had been from Jens' personal files. Among all his notes and research papers had been a complete dossier on her. He'd documented every experiment. Every reaction. His successes and his failures. She hadn't read it, and never intended to, but buried among the details of her nightmare had been some unexpected news.

Her batch-brothers, Hunter and Chase, hadn't abandoned her. They'd kept looking, asking questions and causing problems until they'd finally gotten too close to the truth. Someone had sent an assassin to eliminate them, and they'd died before they could find her. The assassin had been another cyborg, a product of another branch of research—someone like Shadow. River didn't want to know who had done it. Whoever it was, they'd been as much a victim as the rest of them. She hoped that wherever they were, they were free and at peace.

There had been one more piece of information, too. One that had ramifications for every cyborg in existence. Jens and several others had not been content to simply implant codes to control their creations. They'd been experimenting with hardware that could do the same thing. He'd implanted one such device in River. His original message to her had included a signal that activated her implant. That's how he'd tracked her.

There was no record of him ever working on Edge, but one of his fellow researchers must have placed one in Edge at some point. When Jens had broadcast the signal meant to incapacitate River, he'd knocked out Edge instead.

They had sent warnings out to every sector of the galaxy, starting with Haven. A new set of scans would have to be employed to detect the devices, and then they'd need to find a way to remove them.

Edge's hand on her arm brought her out of her

reverie, and his gentle kiss told her he knew what she'd been thinking about.

"Chance is here," he told her. "You okay?"

"Yeah. Just processing," she told him. Edge had been the only one she trusted to read the file and give her what information she should know. The rest, he'd kept to himself, protecting her from reliving the worst years of her life in her quest for the answers she needed.

"Hello!" Chance arrived at their table, beaming. She was a different female than the one River remembered. Unlike most of the cyborgs, Chance hadn't been able to cope with life under an open sky. After spending her entire life as a captive on a space station, living on a planet, or even entering large spaces put her in a state of panic.

Living on Haven had been hell for her. The Drift gave her everything she needed to be happy, including the love of a good man and a job that let her strike back at the bastards who had hurt them all so badly.

River stood to greet her, wrapping the other cyborg in a long hug. "It's good to see you."

"It's wonderful to see you both." Chance flashed Edge an uncertain smile. "Hi, Edge."

He shocked everyone at the table by standing and giving Chance a hug of his own.

By the time they all took their seats, Chance was looking a little dazed. Since the bar wasn't open yet, they couldn't order food or drinks, but it provided a safe place for them to talk without being overheard.

"Do you have any news?" River asked, speaking so softly only another cyborg could hear.

"I do. We have them," Chance said.

Edge frowned. "We've heard that before."

"I know, but you've never heard it from me. I can tell you with ninety-seven percent certainty that the worst of the danger has passed. While threats to Haven will remain, they won't come from Torex or the Shadows. Not in any meaningful way. They've met with too many failures and lost far too much money. They'll move on to other targets now. I'm not saying there won't be more attempts to disrupt the colony, but they don't have the resources to be a true threat. I believe that Haven is safe."

River exhaled sharply. That was good news. Better than she'd hoped for... but she needed to know something else.

"What about our petition?"

Beside her, Edge tensed as he waited for Chance's reply.

The cyborg grinned at them, happier than River had ever seen her. "It's approved! I have the information right here." She placed a data stick on the table. "I asked to be the one to give you this news. I wanted to tell you myself. Everything you need is recorded on here." She tapped the tab. "Copies will be sent to all parties later today. This is it! The cyborgs of Haven colony are no longer confined to the planet. We're all free to go anywhere we want."

Chance chuckled. "I'm not wrong very often, but I'm glad I was this time. I really thought it would take several more years for them to change their minds. I didn't know about Dr. Jens, though. His obsession with you changed the variables."

River leaned over and gave Chance a one-armed hug. "I am so happy! This means you're going to have visitors. You're a big deal back home, you know. The one that got away."

Edge picked up the data stick. "Everything we've wanted is all in here? We're free?"

"Free," Chance agreed.

For a few minutes, they celebrated, asking questions and rejoicing in the news.

Eventually, the subject moved to new topics.

"So, what will the two of you do now?" Chance asked.

River laughed at her. "Why are you asking us? You already know the answer."

Chance shook her head. "I can only calculate probabilities. There are only two beings who can decide what comes next for you." She smiled softly at them. "I just hope that whatever you do, you're happy."

"That much I am certain about," Edge declared. He took River's hand in his and then kissed her softly. "We're going home. I've been told it's time for me to settle down and find something else to do with my life besides telling other cyborgs what to do."

With a heart full of love, River looked at her mate and grinned. "That's not what I said. I suggested that you don't need to be their commander anymore."

"But?" he prompted her, his eyes gleaming now.

"But no matter what happens. You will always be *my* commander."

"And that is all I'll ever need."

River looked around the bar. It was still under

construction, but it was already full of promise, just like Haven.

It was time to go home and discover the life she'd been waiting for—the one with Edge by her side.

***

Thank you for reading Her Cyborg Commander.

I hope you enjoyed Edge and River's story.
Would you like to read a special bonus epilogue to this story? Sign up for my newsletter here:
subscribepage.io/Bonuscontent

If you're looking for more stories like this one, I invite you to explore the other books in the <u>Drift</u> universe, which now Include Haven Colony, <u>Nova Force</u> and the original <u>Drift</u> series.

ABOUT THE AUTHOR

USA Today Bestselling author and writer of award-winning Sci-Fi and Paranormal Romance, Susan recently moved from the wilds of western Canada to the southern coast of Australia. These days she writes from her new home where her every word is scrutinized by her step-lizards and her coffee mug is kept full by her beloved husband.

To contact her about her books or to ask her about her new life in Australia, you can email her at susan@susanhayes.ca or find her at susanhayes.ca. If you'd prefer to stalk her from afar, you can sign up for her newsletter http://susanhayes.ca/susans-newsletter/